When the Grass Is Rising

A Portrait of Young Sam Houston

A Novel

Rose Gonsoulin

Reed & Wright

Early 19th Century American Frontier - Sam Houston - Cherokee Territory - Andrew Jackson - Battle of Horseshoe Bend - 1805 to 1814 Time Period

Reed & Wright, LLC
ISBN: 978-1-73303526-2

Cover Artist: Lesia T. @ Germancreative
Cover photo - subinpumsom

For my mother, Frances…

Sam Houston
March 2, 1793 - July 26, 1863

Political Career

U.S. Congressman, 7th District, Tennessee
1823 - 1827 (two consecutive terms)

Governor, Tennessee
1828 - 1829

President, The Republic of Texas
1836-1838, 1841-1844

U. S. Senator, Texas
1846 - 1859

Governor, Texas
1859 - 1861

Foreword

Historical fiction is an odd duck, especially biographical fiction. Readers are never quite certain when, in service of a likeable protagonist and the three-act structure, the author has embellished the facts, drastically altered them, or disregarded a historical record entirely. When I started this story, I knew I would have to create much of Sam's early life. Save a handful of legends, very little hard evidence of him exists from before 1813. This is why the best nonfiction biographers—James Haley, Marquis James, M. K. Wisehart, and Marshall DeBruhl— offer only a few broad brushstrokes about Sam's teenage years. He runs away and lives with the Cherokee, he pays off his debts by teaching school when he hadn't spent more than six months in a classroom, and he enlists in the infantry and nearly dies in the Battle of Horseshoe Bend.

It's a thrilling adventure based on hearsay and word of mouth. But I needed more to set the scene. I searched in all the usual places: online, libraries, and special collections, including the National Archives. Thousands of source documents on Sam exist, including four volumes of his correspondence. James Haley said writing his biography of Sam took fifteen years because a new cache of letters kept popping up every few years. Yet only scant evidence of his formative years exists.

I started out with scenes of Sam skipping school, fishing with Jerry up Sheep Creek, and fidgeting during Sunday meetings at the Old Stone Church, yet nothing sounded authentic. I didn't feel Sam with me. This sounds silly, but it became a serious roadblock until I visited Forest Oaks, a bed-and-breakfast south of Lexington, Virginia. The original structure was built around 1805 by Matthew Houston, Sam's first cousin once removed.

From there, I went to the Rockbridge County Courthouse, where I found the earliest reference to Sam, his name in his father's will. He was there between Paxton and William and the three younger sisters. Then I saw Sam as the classic middle child, literally and figuratively. Undisciplined and disobedient, reckless at times, Sam was smart but moody, with a preference for reading and an aversion to hard work. How he must have chafed against the strict Presbyterian upbringing imposed upon him.

After the stay at Forest Oaks, each time I hit another stumbling block, I went in search of some historical tidbit to add authenticity to

Sam's story. And something always turned up. One time, it was Doug Winiarski's article about the lawsuits between Sam's father and the Lyles. Rooted in fact, the event on August 4, 1805, not only offered an opening but also brought insight into the Houston household and the character of his father.

A quarter of the way into the first draft, I couldn't move the story forward. Something wasn't right. Turns out the historians have been repeating an error in the birth order of the family. The mistake originated in the biographical account of the Houston family written by Sam's cousin, Reverend Samuel Rutherford Houston. Evidence of the real birth order resides in John Paxton's will, the maternal grandfather.

The strangest moment came just after I felt I'd found the full shape of Sam's story. I luxuriated in the moment, musing about how Sam had often declared to his family, likely in reaction to their scorn or ridicule, that they would one day *hear his name*. That was his way of expressing the profound sense of destiny he felt. Then it came to me—the very first word spoken when man landed on the moon was "Houston." The whole world heard his name that night, but they didn't really know him or his character.

As I considered whether that was irony or destiny, I gazed out the windows at the wide Sonoran desert in our backyard. What I thought was a Harris hawk—I could tell from the white band on its tail feathers—was flying in the distance. But, no, it couldn't be a Harris hawk because the white I saw was the head feathers of a bald eagle. Within seconds, the eagle was coming straight at me. Only a few yards before it reached the window, the eagle swooped up and soared over the roof.

With a chill, I remembered that after saying "Houston," Neil Armstrong announced, "The *Eagle* has landed."

My dear readers, you decide—was that a message from Sam or just happenstance?

Historical Houston Household
(Age in 1805)

Major Samuel Davidson Houston (60)
Elizabeth Blair Paxton Houston (48)
    James (23)
    John (20)
    Robert (18)
    Paxton (15)
    Sam (12)
    William (10)
    Isabella (9)
    Polly (8)
    Eliza (5)

Granny Peg (36)
    Lucy (18)
      Andrew (1)
    Jerry (12)

Historical Cherokee

Oolooteka, aka John Jolly – chief of Hiwassee Island

Tahlonteeskee – older brother to Oolooteka and

chief of Cayoka village

Hell Jack Fire – white trader, father of John Rogers and Tiana Rogers

John Rogers – son of Hell Jack Fire and his first Cherokee wife

Doublehead – uncle or great uncle to Oolooteka and Tahlonteeskee

Tsali – The Prophet

The Ridge, aka Major Ridge – prominent Cherokee chief

Toutcheelengh – chief of Willstown

Black Fox – Most Beloved Man of Cherokee People

The Glass, aka Virginia Tom – Cherokee chief prominently featured in Norton's journal

Pathkiller, aka John Lowry – Cherokee chief

Turtle-at-Home – Cherokee chief prominently featured in Norton's journal

Rising Fawn, aka George Lowry – Cherokee chief

Big Acorn – fictional name given to a warrior featured in Norton's journal

Ground Squirrel – fictional name given to Oolooteka's wife

Tecumseh – famous Shawnee chief

Glossary

Ball Play – a game similar to lacrosse played by the Cherokee men.

Beeves – beef cows.

Brain-tanned – the use of the brains of a deer as a softening agent on hide while making leather.

Brooksies – a slang term for brook trout.

Chicicoos - small turtle shells filled with pebbles and strapped to the knees. Cherokee women wore them during dances to create sound.

Doplic – Pennsylvania Dutch term meaning "clumsy."

Driver – a Cherokee referee in the ball play tournaments.

Frizzen – L-shaped hammer used in flintlock firearms.

Granny hole – a small window in a schoolhouse positioned near the schoolmaster's desk.

Going to water – a term for the ritual cleansing in the river before a Ball Play tournament.

Gorget – a half-moon-shaped necklace made of metal. It was first worn as a piece of armor to protect the throat. Later, gorgets were worn as ornaments in ceremonial costumes.

Indian Family – a family that did not attend church service.

Lazy board – a bench at the rear of a wagon for someone to sit and work the brake, if needed.

Linkster – slang for translator.

Rutschy – Pennsylvania Dutch term meaning "fidgeting" or "restless."

Stripers – slang for striped bass.

Chapter One

"Put the book away," Ma said.

Sam couldn't take his eyes off the page. "But Robinson Crusoe just discovered a footprint in the sand."

Someone suddenly ripped the book from Sam's hands and whacked him on the head with it. Laughing, John held it out of reach. Sam's brother was five inches taller and thirty pounds heavier. Lowering his head like a bull, Sam rammed John in the chest, and the book fell to the floor. He quickly retrieved it.

"Don't hit your brother," his father said.

Ma cast a stern eye on John then nodded to Sam with the slightest smile. "Both of you come to the table."

Before Sam could move, Major Houston yelled, "Boy, do as you're told or I will whip your backside!"

His brother smacked Sam on the head again. "Obey the Major."

"John shouldn't be taunting him," his mother said.

His father scoffed loudly. "You coddle that boy too much, Elizabeth."

Sam took his seat at the table between James and John, where he never had enough elbow room. He put the book in his lap and sat up very straight and tall, trying to look as prim and proper as possible, hoping to make his mother smile.

"John, take that blasted book from him," his father said.

But James was the one who snatched it away and handed it over to Ma. She set it near the milk jug. Then she caught Sam's eye, giving him the slightest nod. The book would be safe for the time being.

Too often, just to be mean and spiteful, John would hide whatever Sam was reading.

If his two oldest brothers weren't abusing him, they were ignoring him. By the time Sam was born, the alliances between his four older brothers had already become set in stone. James and John were an arrogant pair, lording their seniority over everyone else. The next in line, Robert and Paxton, were steadfast friends, supporting each other against James and John.

Sam's younger brother, William, should have been a natural ally, but he had a meek manner and was almost three years younger, while Sam was twelve, going on thirteen. He didn't want to spend time with a baby. If not for Jerry, Sam wouldn't have any true friend in the family. Of course, to the others, Jerry didn't count as a strong ally because he was a Negro.

Jerry counted to Sam, though. They were close in age and had grown up in each other's company. For some time, Sam had thought Jerry was his brother. One night when Sam was much younger, he tried to go sleep with Jerry in the servants' quarters, a small shack behind the house. Ma explained that although Jerry was part of their family, he came from a different side. She finally convinced Sam that Jerry had his own house, just like their cousins lived in their own houses, and everybody needed to sleep in their own room. Sam believed it at the time, but later, he came to understand the real reason he wasn't supposed to treat Jerry like a brother. His mother hadn't lied, but she'd not told the whole story, either. So for friends that counted in the eyes of his family, Sam had to look to his cousins who lived near Timber Ridge.

His mother bowed her head, the signal for their father to give the blessing.

With a voice harsh and raspy, Major Samuel Houston mumbled a familiar prayer. Lately, his father's nose seemed redder and bumpier, and the blue spider veins across his cheeks were more prominent.

Sunday dinners were always a cold meal, for even the slaves weren't supposed to labor much on the Sabbath. Two dozen smoked brook trout and three eel pies, the last of Saturday's saddle of mutton, beef tongue with dressed cucumbers, a bowl of boiled potatoes and carrots, pickles, wheat bread, potted cheese, and pears and gooseberries filled the middle of the long oak table.

Major Houston picked up a large knife with its matching fork and carved slices from the mutton. Platters, plates, and bowls passed in a steady rotation, following the unspoken rule of one heaping spoonful apiece until all were served.

"Elizabeth, I'll need the hemp when I leave tomorrow," his father said.

As an inspector for the Virginia Militia, Major Houston often traveled the countryside. With his father away, the family would settle into a more relaxed routine, and Ma always seemed to have more time to listen to Sam.

"I gave it to Pastor Blain," his mother answered then quietly added, "Elder Lyle said we were late with our giving."

"Samuel Lyle has no right to talk to my wife about church business."

"He spoke with me." Paxton was three years older than Sam and the only redhead in the family.

"You should have told him to wait until the tobacco comes in." His father picked at a piece of gristle between his teeth.

"We won't fill a hogshead this year," Robert said.

Major Houston licked his fingers. "If you were all pulling your weight, maybe we'd have a better crop."

The past year had been harder because their best worker, Boatswain, had been sold to a man in Staunton. Only Jerry remained to help with the farm, so everyone was expected to do more.

"Sam didn't clean out the corn crib like he was supposed to." John took the last piece of eel pie.

Sam turned to his mother. "If I hadn't gone fishing, we wouldn't be eating these brooksies for dinner."

Isabella came into the dining room. Sam's sister had a crippled gait and an elongated face with droopy eyes and was small for her age. She hobbled to Ma's side, babbling nonsense.

"Where's that wench, Peggy? She should be watching the girl," the Major said.

"I gave Peggy the afternoon to tend her garden."

"The child smells of sour milk and soiled linen. Take her away, Elizabeth!"

Seeing a chance to escape the afternoon meeting, Sam jumped from his seat.

"No." The Major directed his ire at Sam. "You'll not use this as an excuse to disappear."

Sam sank back into the chair, and Ma rose and shepherded Isabella out of the room.

In her absence, the Major said, "I can't imagine how loose and idle the servants are when I am away. It's your mother's poor management that is causing our ruin."

"Ma works harder than anybody else," Sam said.

"Do not contradict the Major," John said.

"Just keep your mouth shut." James stabbed the last bite of mutton on Sam's plate.

"That's mine!"

"Not anymore." James pushed the meat into his mouth.

"Sir," Paxton said, drawing everyone's attention, "Mr. Kinneer says we need to restore our fields with clover. His wheat crop is twice as tall as ours."

"John Kinneer could talk the hind leg off a donkey about his clover," the Major said.

James talked while chewing. "Clover don't pay a penny's worth."

"What if we could grow four-leaf clover." Sam laughed. "I bet that's worth a lot of money."

"You're an idiot." The Major rolled his eyes and shook his head.

Paxton smiled at Sam.

"What are you smirking at? If you and that one"—his father darted his eyes in Sam's direction but never actually looked at him—"don't start working harder, I may have to resign my commission."

"Major, no. You can't quit the militia," John cried.

His father puffed up his chest. "It's men like Mr. Kinneer who should be doing more to keep the country safe from the savages and the Tories. But he stays home to count his coin."

"It's true," John said. "The miserly coward wants the comfort of his hearth while braver men like my father are away protecting our land."

"But if we can't grow a decent crop, it stands to reason to try," Paxton said.

Sam admired Paxton for speaking up in spite of the withering stare from their father.

The Major pounded a fist on the table. "If gold is all you want, then we could buy a still and sell whiskey."

Ma came into the room, and the table went silent. Once settled, she picked up her fork, prongs pointed upward. In her firmest voice, she said slowly, calmly, "I will not allow my sons to be led astray and turned into fools, sots, and gamblers." Lowering her chin, she looked the Major in the eye from across the table. "There will never be spirits-making in my house."

"It suited your father," the Major grumbled under his breath, just loudly enough for Sam to hear.

Ma pursed her lips tightly.

After a few moments, the Major said, "That was a fine sermon this morning, Elizabeth. It gave me pleasure to hear the old psalms again. We should invite Pastor Heron to visit more often."

"But he sounds like a horse when he sings. Hee, haw, hee, haw." Sam turned to his mother, mimicking the pastor.

Ma had a slight smile on her lips when she said, "That's enough, Sam."

"I like the new hymns better." Sam threw his head back, closed his eyes, and sang, "Judges, who rule the world by laws, will ye despise the righteous cause?"

A sting at the back of his head made Sam stop. When John tried to smack him again, Sam recoiled, bumping against James, who then shoved Sam from the other side.

"Sam, there's no singing at the table," his mother said.

John gave a sly eye to Sam then turned to their father. "Sam was hoping Ann Henderson would go into one of her fits."

Sam couldn't suppress a laugh. "She flops around like a fish sometimes." He swung his head from side to side and waved his hands in the air.

The Major slammed a fist against the table, this time rattling the silverware. "Boy, you're no better than those Kentucky jerkers. I've a mind to send you to live with an Indian family for the disrespect you show in Sunday meetings."

A smart retort sat on the tip of his tongue, but Sam knew he'd gone too far this time. He shrank back into his chair.

The Major scanned the table with a scowl on his face. At least his father's anger wasn't directed solely at Sam anymore.

"Pastor Blain has been too tolerant with that girl." White froths of spittle flew from his father's mouth. "It's blasphemy what those jerkers are doing. It has no place at Sunday meetings."

The Major grabbed the silver-edged carving knife and stabbed it into the table. Not even John would speak up when their father flew into a rage, as had been happening more often over the past few months.

"My dear husband," Ma said in her sweet voice. "I ask you not to ruin my finest cutlery. It's the only gift I have left from my father."

In the silence, flies landed freely on the bits of food not eaten.

After a moment, Robert rose from his seat, breaking the tension. Just when Paxton appeared ready to follow, Robert said, "Martha McChesney is returning to Brownsburg today." He bobbed his head and made for the door.

Soon the others left, but Sam remained seated, hoping to retrieve his book and sneak in a little more reading before the service began.

But Paxton waited at the open door and said, "Sam, come on."

Sparrows were scavenging on the front step. Together, Sam and Paxton walked down a narrow lane lined with black locust and white oaks. A stern wind swept through the trees, rustling the leaves and carrying an early hint of autumn.

"When did Mr. Kinneer tell you about the clover?" Sam asked.

"Ma sent me to borrow some flour last week." Paxton stopped then turned to face their house. "Did you know that when the Major's father built this place, it was the finest in the county, the first to have glass panes."

Sam looked at their two-story brick home. The roof leaked under a heavy rain, and the chimney in the keeping room didn't draw well anymore.

"You see Thorn Hill, the cornfield beneath it?" Paxton squinted into the afternoon sun and pointed to the northeast. "That was part of Grandfather's farm too."

Sam gazed out on the green pastures and soft yellowing meadows. After a moment, he asked, "Well, how come it's not ours now?"

"The Major sold it."

"Why?"

"Same reason he sold Boatswain. He needed the money. No telling how much is wasted when he's out making his inspections, mostly in the taverns."

Paxton rested his hand on Sam's shoulder. His brother was several inches taller and had a slender, wiry frame. Of all his brothers, Paxton was the most energetic and full of vitality, the only one who dared to challenge the Major.

"All that's left of Ma's inheritance is Granny Peg. The Major would have sold her, too, if he could have."

"Ma wouldn't let him."

"You know why, don't you?"

Sam shrugged.

"Granny Peg is Ma's kin."

"What? How can that be?"

A sly smile crossed Paxton's face. "The boar don't care if the sow is black or white, does he?"

Sam stood silent, stunned and confused. Granny Peg did have light skin and freckles and soft gray eyes, like his mother. Her children, Lucy and Jerry, were dark, but not the deep coal black like Boatswain. Sam knew how making babies worked, but only recently had he begun to imagine it for humans, for himself. The idea of his parents, though—ugh, disgusting, impossible.

"Isn't it wrong to call girls pigs?" Sam asked.

"That's how Robert heard it. 'It's the boar's nature to mount the sow in heat' is what Uncle John told him." Paxton paused. "Anyway, you can't just read the Bible. You have to look at the barnyard to see how the world really works."

"Who was it?" Sam asked.

Paxton glanced down then looked up at the sky. "Nobody knows for certain, but Robert said everyone believes it was Uncle John."

"The one who said that about the boar?"

Paxton nodded.

A vague sense came to Sam that there existed a world around him he could neither see nor understand. That thought brought on a strange sensation, at once familiar but haunting and deeply disturbing, as though a dark and sinister world lurked in the shadows around him. He couldn't see it, but he sensed its presence. Instinctively, Sam glanced over his shoulder at the Old Stone Church, where the other families were packing up after their Sunday dinners, folding blankets, and tending horses. The scene was so common and simple and good that he wondered how this bizarre other world could exist alongside normal, everyday life yet stay hidden.

"Robert only thinks about Martha McChesney now. James has no plans to strike out on his own even though he's twenty-one. Neither he nor John has the gumption to leave. The Major will certainly give Timber Ridge to John."

Paxton acted as if they had all afternoon to spare and had never shared a confidence like that before. Two ravens frolicked on the wind, dipping and diving, squawking as they flew by.

"Why does the Major treat me so bad?" Sam asked.

Paxton sighed. "You won't remember, but when he was promoted to Major, he demanded we stop calling him Pa. William wasn't born yet. Ma caught him whipping you because you kept calling him Pa. It's the only time I ever saw her raising a hand against him."

They started walking again, nearing the wagon road. The summer sun beat down on the old Indian trace, a path carved out long before by the Cherokee, Iroquois, and Shawnee. Through a dusty haze, a large covered wagon approached. A pair of oxen lumbered by, their hooves kicking up puffs from the dry earth.

"Robert and I are supposed to be leaving together, to go west, where the land is practically free." Paxton coughed from the dust and waited for the wagon to pass. "But now, he says he doesn't want to leave Virginia because of Martha McChesney."

The dust settled, and the wagon disappeared as the road began the descent into Lexington, where a knot of the old traces converged to cross the North River.

Paxton started toward the Old Stone Church. "I'm not sticking around like James and John. There won't be anything left when I come of age."

"Can I come with you?" Sam asked.

"You'll need your own rifle."

The church doors remained open in the heat of summer, leaving the hounds to wander in and out as they pleased. Maybe Sam would get lucky and a dogfight would interrupt the afternoon meeting.

As they entered, a church elder handed Paxton a token but had nothing for Sam. The very last part of Sunday meeting was reserved for the communion table. Only the devout and pious were invited to receive a blessing of bread and vinegar. Sam had never been given a token, but that didn't bother him because neither had William nor his cousin Tom Letcher. They weren't old enough.

Sam and Paxton took their places in the family pew, second from the front. The Major sat by the center aisle, with Elizabeth then the three girls—Isabella, Polly, and Eliza—beside her. Next were the sons, seated in order of birth. Sam sat between Paxton and William.

William was holding a token. What? Did Tom Letcher get one too? Sam craned his neck around to see if he could catch his cousin's attention, but the assembly rose to their feet when Reverend Blain climbed into the pulpit. After a quarter hour of praying for God's blessing on their worship, an elder read the Scripture of the day.

"A reading from Matthew twenty-five, verse thirty-three: 'And the Lord shall set the sheep on his right hand but the goats on the left.'"

From his perch, Reverend Blain raised his arms high and wide.

"Who among us are sheep, and who are goats? The sheep shall be given eternal life under God's divine grace, but to the goats, the Lord shall say, 'Depart from me, you cursed. Go to the eternal fire prepared for the devil and his angels.'"

The pastor paused. "How will God choose, you may ask?" His eyes roved over the congregation and seemed to narrow as they rested on Sam.

Sam shifted in his seat.

"'Tis not yours to question." The pastor's voice rose to a high pitch, and he pointed a finger toward the sky. "Mere humans must recognize God's hand is divine and accept His arbitrary choice. As Peter says in chapter three, verse seventeen, 'For it is far better to suffer for doing good if that should be God's will. But suffer you must be willing to do, to do it gladly for all eternity.'"

A black hound dog strolled up the center aisle then stopped to scratch its ear.

"The devil waits and watches, knowing the seeds of evil reside in every man's heart. We are all sinners. For any hope of salvation, you must be willing to endure the exquisite misery of hell, not for days or years, but for the longest forever, a boundless duration which will swallow up your thoughts, and you will absolutely lose hope of ever having any deliverance from hell."

The reverend cast his eyes around the room and landed on Sam once more as though he were talking directly to him. Sam crossed his arms against his chest.

"This dungeon of eternal damnation will be tight and narrow, to bind all those who refused to be bound by God's law, the damned souls heaped together in darkness, scratching and gouging at their eyeballs, gnawing on their own tongues…"

The image struck fear in Sam's heart, and gooseflesh rose on his arms.

"A fire that emits no light but boils their blood and enflames their bowels."

A sudden panic overcame Sam. *What if God has already decided I'm going to hell, no matter how good I try to be?* The injustice tormented him as the pastor droned on.

"The stench of rotting flesh fouls the air. The tortured souls rage at each other, howling and screaming blasphemies while the devil mocks and jeers them. The punishment will be infinite despair and wretchedness. Amen."

Reverend Blain descended from the pulpit, and Sam exhaled deeply. He felt a sense of relief but was still troubled that God could be so hateful and arbitrary.

The precentor rose to lead the congregation in song. The selection was a favorite because it had a rhythm that invited swaying. Sam sang with gusto and joy, the music carrying him away from the prospect of damnation.

When a loud erratic clapping came from the back pew, Sam turned eagerly and saw young Ann Henderson standing with her hands high above her head. As she moved to the center aisle, her head twitched and jerked. She stopped in a sliver of sunlight coming through the door, and without warning, the girl began to spin in a tight circle, sending the small hat she wore to the wooden floor. She stomped on it, and her singing became a shrill and harsh gibberish.

Sam's father sprang to his feet and lurched toward the girl. Ann didn't seem to notice when the Major grabbed her by the shoulders, commanding her, "Stop at once."

The girl thrashed and bucked against the Major's hold.

A woman cried out, "It's the Holy Spirit that's entered her."

"It is blasphemy!" the Major yelled in response.

Samuel Lyle, the most respected elder in the congregation, slowly stood from his position in the front pew.

"Major Houston, you are the one disrupting the dignity and peace of our assembly. Allow the girl her freedom."

Reverend Blain stepped forward a few feet. "Brother Houston, time will tell soon enough if the Holy Spirit stays with the child. Only God can know for certain. It is not ours to judge."

As though in retort, Ann thrust her chin up and barked out a string of high-pitched yelps, setting the hounds outside to howling.

The Major forcibly dragged the young girl out the front door.

Reverend Blain returned to the pulpit. As though nothing had happened, he called out, "All rise, and let us continue our worship."

John rose quickly from his seat and trampled over Robert, Paxton, Sam, and William to reach the side aisle. He rushed out the front door. Taking advantage of the commotion, Sam stepped from the pew and hurried to the side door. He intended to seek the peace and tranquility of the wooded hills but couldn't leave without taking Robinson Crusoe with him.

He went directly to their house and snuck in through the back door. The dining room was cloaked in a dim light. Sam found the book in his mother's chair. He picked it up and was about to leave but stopped when he heard voices from the parlor. With a furtive glance through the doorway, Sam saw his father and John with Ann Henderson.

His father had the girl pinned in a chair. "Settle down, and behave."

Ann squirmed and tried to free herself, but John grabbed a fistful of her hair. She cried out when he jerked her head back.

Sam stepped forward. "You're hurting her!"

His father turned toward Sam. "Get back to church."

John snarled at Sam, baring his teeth. "We're teaching her a lesson."

Sam felt blood rise to his face as his cheeks grew hot. He rushed toward John and started punching him. His brother let go of the girl's hair to strike at Sam.

The Major grabbed Sam and shook him, shouting, "How dare you defy me!"

The girl jumped from the chair, and John caught her around the waist. She squirmed and tried to get away, but he kept a tight hold. The Major was still holding Sam's arm and glared down with a twisted smile on his lips as he raised his other hand. But before his father could land a blow, Sam jerked free of his grip. He didn't run off, though. Instead, he stood his ground.

"I have a name. It's the same as yours. Why can't you ever say it?"

"Since the day you were born, you've been a vain, feckless child, always full of your own importance."

All the animosity and disdain Sam ever sensed while in his father's presence lay at his feet, like stones cast at an offender. His cheeks burned, and he clenched his fists, but Sam wasn't injured or intimidated. Rather, he felt relief because his father's hatred was out in the open where Sam could see it for what it was—jealous, small-minded, petty, and spiteful.

"Know this: one day, when people hear about Sam Houston, it will be me they think of, not you, Pa."

The Major's face froze as though he'd seen a ghost. John started for Sam, but he bolted from the room. His heart pounded against his ribs, and he didn't stop running until he reached the rise that marked their property line with the Lyle's farm. As he caught his breath, hands at his waist, he knew he would pay for his insolence, but he didn't care. Paxton was his friend now. And he would always have his mother's love and affection. He didn't need his father. And if God was as harsh and arbitrary in his judgments as it appeared, then maybe Sam didn't need God either.

He stayed away all night. The air was warm, and he made a bed of boughs stripped from the trunk of a pine tree. Sam lay awake in the comfort of the fresh green scent with the crickets and frogs and night birds to keep him company, dreaming of the day he and Paxton would leave Timber Ridge.

Chapter Two

"The feed buckets are empty," Ma said.

The bed of the buckboard wagon held a stack of blankets and baskets of food. Granny Peg, Polly, and Eliza were seated atop the blankets.

"William was supposed to fill them before he left." Sam folded his arms across his chest. "I had to hitch and load the wagon by myself today."

His mother shook her head in exasperation. "Son, you don't do your fair share when your brothers are here. It's only right you shoulder a bigger load while they're away."

"One hundred percent is not a share. It's the whole pie! I thought you were better at ciphering, Ma." Sam drew his eyes wide in mock astonishment.

Typically, that would produce a chuckle from his mother, but not that day.

"You've been bellyaching for two days straight. I thought you'd be tired of it by now."

"But Ma, why did William get to go instead of me? It was my turn."

Tradition said that, at his age, Sam would be the one selected as the Major's aide-de-camp for the annual Muster and Roll Call. Paxton had done it the last few years and Robert before him. Sam had been certain his turn would come this year.

"You had your chance last year when you were supposed to be the aide for your brothers. They said you never came around."

"All they wanted me for was to fetch their water."

"Well, I asked the Major to let you stay with me. William can't do as much as you can."

Sam didn't believe her, knowing full well how his father felt toward him. "Why didn't you at least have me go with Cousin Matthew?"

"I have my reasons. Now, fill those buckets."

"Promise me I get to join the muster next year. Please."

"Only the Lord knows what will happen next year. Hurry up."

With a loud sigh, Sam took the two feed buckets into the barn.

Last year's muster had been the most exciting time of Sam's life. He and his cousin Tom had roamed the militia camp together. They watched the soldiers practice their line formations, the men marching and wheeling about with the mounted officers dashing to and fro, calling out commands. But this year, he was trapped. It rankled Sam sorely, yet he could do nothing about it. Complaining only brought more ridicule from his brothers.

He filled each bucket with a mixture of oats and wheat chaff and hung them on the hooks under the wagon bed. Then, when he hiked a leg up to the running board, he heard and felt his breeches split. He turned and saw his faded drawers exposed by a large rip in the center seam.

"Ma, I told you I needed new breeches."

"Where are the breeches I made for your birthday?"

"They're too small now."

Many nights that summer, Sam's legs had ached as he lay in bed, trying to fall asleep. And he seemed to be hungry all the time. It wasn't his fault that he'd gotten taller and bigger almost overnight.

"There's a larger pair in the trunk by the trundle bed."

"But Ma, those breeches have more patches on them than a quilt. Everybody else has nice clothes, but I might as well wrap myself in a dirty old blanket, and you don't even care." Sam locked his arms tight against his chest and declared, "I won't go into town unless I have on decent clothes!"

"You'll just have to make do with what we have." Ma slid over on the bench seat, taking the reins firmly in hand. She let out the brake, but before giving a flick of the reins, she turned to Sam. "Do not fall into one of your melancholy spells today. I need you to unload the wagon and tend to the horses. You can meet us on Mulberry Hill."

Then she gave a hard snap with the reins and drove off without a backward glance. He couldn't believe she would leave him. Sam sulked toward the house, kicking any small rocks in his path. If he didn't hurry, he would miss the parade, but the excitement and anticipation had turned into a lump of lead in the pit of his stomach. He would be dressed in rags, which was terribly unfair because all the others had received new militia uniforms—buckskin breeches, indigo-dyed hunting shirts with red fringe at the yoke, wool jackets, tow-linen knapsacks, and a low-crowned hat with a small black cockade. Sam had received nothing, but his older brothers got blankets oiled to repel the rain and leather girdles fashioned to carry a cartridge box, knife, bayonet, tomahawk, and tin canteen.

And his mother had made a new uniform for the Major too. That year, Colonel Barbour had commanded that officers wear white cuffs and gold epaulets with a bright-red sash across the waist. For months, his sisters, Polly and Eliza, had carded the wool while Ma sat at her spindle, working the fluffy piles into thread. Then she wove the threads on her loom, and late in the evenings, she stitched under the faint light of a tallow candle while Sam read to her from the Bible.

Granny Peg and her daughter, Lucy, had made knee-high moccasins with the brain-tanned deerskins purchased from Cousin Matthew's general store. And each of Sam's older brothers carried a musket. At least William hadn't been given a gun before Sam received his.

And everyone but Sam would be in the parade too. At noon, Colonel Barbour would lead the Eighth Regiment up Main Street then out to Mulberry Hill, next to the old Liberty Hall ruins, where a feast fit for a king waited—pies and cakes, roasted nuts, peach preserves, fresh bread with apple butter and cheese, venison, roasted pig, corn, and plenty of cider. Not that Sam was allowed to drink cider.

Since dawn, the wagon road had been busy with families flowing toward Lexington. His father's first cousin, Matthew Houston, had arrived from Vine Oaks the day before. He brought his wife, Patsy, their infant son, and the three other children, all under the age of ten. A young Irish girl working off a seven-year indenture came with them too. Having the houseguests meant the room where all the brothers slept had been given over to Cousin Matthew and his family.

Sam stood at the back door, tempted to run off. A fly circled and landed on his cheek. He swatted at it and went inside, trudging up the stairs. When Sam walked into the bedroom, Cousin Patsy had the baby to her breast. The shock of it sent him out of the room.

A few seconds later, Cousin Patsy called to him, "It's all right now. You can come in."

The servant girl was holding up a large sheet, shielding Patsy but blocking Sam's access to the trunk.

"Sorry, Cousin Patsy. I need to fetch some breeches."

Sam heard a quick rustling noise, and soon, the sheet was down. He went to the old trunk, and the young servant girl giggled as he walked by.

"Yes, I see why you need another pair," Cousin Patsy said politely.

Sam quickly put his hand on his backside, trying to cover the rip, humiliated by having his drawers showing in front of two females, especially Cousin Patsy. She was the youngest and the prettiest wife among the extended family. He lifted the lid, and sure enough, the old breeches were there, patched and stitched up many times over.

Cousin Patsy eyed the raggedy old pair. "Sam, those are too pitiful to wear, and I don't think they'll fit you properly. Come here."

She took the breeches in her hands. "Turn around."

He stood with his back to her and felt her press the breeches against his waist.

"No, these won't do well at all."

"That's all we have," he said.

"Sally, find the extra pair of Mr. Houston's pants. They should do in a pinch."

The young girl pulled a pair of linen pants from a valise on the floor.

"Here, let me see." Cousin Patsy held the pants up to Sam's waist. Her close attention brought on a tingle of pleasure that flooded Sam's body from head to toe. "Yes, these might be a little long, but I think they'll do."

The servant girl lifted the sheet again while Sam changed into the pants.

"Why, those pants fit splendidly." Cousin Patsy smiled and reached to tuck in his shirt at the back. "You have your father's blue eyes, but you've got the look of the Paxton clan."

She took the baby in her arms again.

"When I married Mr. Houston, you were about the same age as my Andrew is now. You'd just found your legs and couldn't be contained. I remember praying to God that He would give me a child as healthy as you."

Hearing he'd been special to someone as a baby changed Sam's attitude. No longer angry at being left behind, he sensed the gloom lifting, and he couldn't wait to show off the long pants.

The sun was a quarter way across the sky when he left Timber Ridge. The sweat on his neck soon disappeared in the cool, crisp air. He ran along the path, passing carts and wagons and horses streaming into town. He didn't stop to talk to neighbors, anxious to follow the smell of campfires and meat cooking on open pits.

The day would be a glorious one after all.

When Sam reached the North River, the distant beat of drums urged him to move faster, for fear the parade had already started. A throng of people packed the narrow toll bridge there. He turned off and scampered down behind Furr's Mill to the low water crossing. He forded the river quickly and scrambled up the bank and took off running. He passed the stocks and pillory, empty because the church elders had voted to let the transgressors out early for the muster.

He went along the north side of Main Street. Crowds lined both sides of the lane. Sam made his way to the Midland Trail, where the militia would turn west and head to the meadow beneath Mulberry Hill. He squeezed into an open space at the front to get a better view.

Leading the column of soldiers, Colonel Barbour sat tall and erect on a dapple-gray charger. His sword was drawn and gleamed in the sunlight. The line advanced, slowly and steadily, the drums beating out time with a rat-tat-tat. A shiver of pure excitement ran down Sam's spine.

Next came the officers of the regiment. Sam's father rode his sorrel mare. Seeing the Major looking brave and majestic touched Sam, and an unexpected tenderness of pride and warmth swept over him. Maybe he did love his father despite their differences.

From somewhere close by, a man with a loud, gruff voice said, "Major Houston has always had a soldierly bearing."

Sam looked around and saw Cousin Matthew's brother, Reverend Houston. He couldn't turn sideways in Rockbridge County without running into a relative.

Through the clatter of voices and the stomp of feet marching by, a clear answer came: "He has a fine military carriage, but he's a fool of a planter. I gave him a fair price…"

Sam leaned forward and saw a neighbor, Mr. Kinneer, standing on the other side of the reverend.

Reverend Houston said, "Too much love for the militia and cider."

A wagon pulling a small cannon rolled by, and Sam couldn't hear Mr. Kinneer's response. He stared ahead as a unit of riflemen approached, but all his senses were keen to the voices of the two men, who had no idea that one of the Major's sons was standing nearby.

The reverend's deep voice was easier to hear. "How many times did the Lyles sue him?"

"Three times," Mr. Kinneer answered.

Sam didn't know about any lawsuits. If there'd been lingering tension with the Lyles over his father's treatment of Ann Henderson, he'd not seen or heard of it. But the Major had been away more than usual over the past year, and Ma wasn't one to talk about squabbles with their neighbors.

Over the rumble of approaching wagons, Reverend Houston said, "James and John are good Presbyterian boys."

The procession of wagons carrying the supplies and provisions for the militia started. Cousin Matthew led three wagons he'd brought from his mill and trading store, packed with saltpeter from the mine at Natural Bridge—his offering in lieu of military service. Next in line, the blacksmith drove a wagon loaded with a cache of muskets and long rifles. As the procession petered out, the voices returned.

Mr. Kinneer said, "The boy Paxton has the most sense."

"Who's the wild one the elders at Timber Ridge are dead set against?"

"That's Sam. No matter how much his brothers thrash him, he runs off to the hills when he should be in the schoolhouse. But he's the favorite with Mrs. Houston."

They're talking about me!

"We'll see him in the pillory one day," Reverend Houston said.

The pillory? What did I ever do to deserve that insult?

The crowd began to move away. Sam stepped forward, facing Reverend Houston and Mr. Kinneer. He thrust his shoulders back and stood as tall as he could. Both men appeared surprised, but Reverend Houston's face quickly softened.

"Why, Samuel, you have shot up a foot since I last saw you." The reverend eyed the long pants Sam wore. "How old are you now?"

"Thirteen, and my name is Sam." He looked at Mr. Kinneer. "Both of you, sirs, shall hear from me again, and it will not be from under the yoke of the pillory."

Sam turned on his heel and dashed off in a fury of emotion. The shock of hearing his name spoken with such derision was like an ill wind at his back. The sharp pang of learning the naked truth of what people thought of him cut deep. The insult to his character troubled him, but he started to question, after making his bold declaration, how he would prove them wrong.

Sam raced by the small camps of those who'd followed husbands, fathers, and sons to the muster. The family wagon stood under a chestnut tree so large that its trunk was the size of a small cabin and hid the view of Gallows Hill in the west. Polly and Eliza were picking the thorny chestnut burrs off the ground.

John and James were there too.

John immediately asked, "Are those my new pants?"

"No."

"Where'd you get them from?"

"They're a pair of Boatswain's old pants," he lied just to provoke his brother.

Sure enough, John came for him, but Sam moved on in search of his mother.

She frowned when she saw him. "I told you to wear the breeches. You were not to wear John's new pants."

"Cousin Patsy said those breeches were too pitiful to wear. She lent me Cousin Matthew's pants."

"Sam, you've contradicted my wishes again." His mother let out a deep sigh and smoothed the folds on her dress.

"Ma, were there lawsuits with the Lyles?"

"Who told you that?"

"I heard Reverend Houston and Mr. Kinneer talking."

His mother pursed her lips tight and leveled her sternest eye at Sam. "It's a sin to eavesdrop." Then she turned her back to him. "Go help Jerry water the horses. And don't come to eat until you've asked the Lord to forgive your sins. All of them."

Her disapproval stung, especially after hearing the prediction that he was destined for the pillory. The world seemed against him that day. He went to help Jerry unhitch the buckboard Ma had driven. Sam took the two roans, and Jerry followed with the big iron-gray mare and the light bay. They headed to Woods Creek, passing a line of the militia, relaxed and gathered in small groups, some in uniform, some not. Excitement filled their voices. Sam slowed to catch snatches of the talk.

"Burr's recruiting soldiers," one man said.

Sam picked out Paxton's red hair. "Paxton!" he yelled.

But his brother didn't notice. He called again, and Paxton glanced his way briefly without acknowledging him. More dejected than ever, Sam walked on. Everyone else got an adventure except him. His mother had turned a cold shoulder to him, he'd missed the muster, and now he felt wounded by Paxton's indifference. Maybe Paxton would abandon their friendship. Maybe he'd found someone else, someone his own age to go off with on his adventure. Sam wanted to drop the lead and leave the horses for Jerry, but he couldn't do that, knowing Jerry would be the one who suffered the consequences.

He tramped on through a field of yellowing corn stubble, harvested but not yet burnt. They soon reached the spring, where crystal-clear water seeped from a slate ledge under the scarlet red of poplar trees. The creek bank was close by. They turned the horses loose. Both boys dropped down and took their fill of the cool drink.

Then Sam leaned back against a beech tree, its trunk covered with soft green moss and turned up in the shape of a chair. He watched a pair of squirrels gathering nuts and the birds pecking at the covering of fallen leaves. Sam stared at the flow of water. For the first time, he noticed how the water zigzagged over the flat slate rocks, making sharp turns at the slightest crack or crevice, like a switchback on a mountain trail.

"Why does everybody think I'm going to end up in jail or somewhere bad?"

"Probably cause you're always causing a ruckus about something."

"Do I complain a lot?"

"Yes sirree, you sure do. Granny Peg says it's cause you're trying to get out of doing any work." Jerry sat on a rock and let the water flow over his bare feet.

"I need my thinking time and my reading time."

"You get lots of that, I know."

"Are you calling me lazy?"

"Don't have to. Everybody does it for me." Jerry smiled.

Sam flicked water with his foot at Jerry. Jerry splashed a little back at him.

"Let's you and me go live in the woods," Sam said. "We can be free men on our own."

"Granny Peg says not to think about that kind of thing." Jerry moved farther into the creek where the water pooled behind a rock. He bent down and wet his hands then rubbed the dark skin on his neck.

Sam sighed loudly. "If I could only live on my own without being ruled or judged by others."

"How would you feed yourself?" Jerry cupped his hands, filled them with water, then dumped it over his head.

"Hunt and fish." Sam picked up a piece of bark fallen from a sycamore tree.

Jerry stood and shook his head, beads of water flying off his thick black hair. "Where would you sleep?"

"Under the trees."

"What about when it gets cold?"

"I'll kill a bear and sleep under the skin."

"Not me. I like where I am. Don't need any freedom. Granny Peg says if I work hard and don't cause no trouble, Miss Elizabeth won't never sell me."

Instantly, Sam regretted his outburst, knowing he shouldn't talk of freedom with Jerry anymore. It was cruel and mean, especially when he thought of Boatswain being sold. He felt more a fool than he'd ever felt when his brothers or father ridiculed him. Jerry was likely

Sam's kin but a slave nonetheless. A memory returned, of the day Boatswain was taken away, about a week after they'd finished the spring planting. Ma had told Sam to take Jerry fishing before the man from Staunton came.

His eyes watered, and Sam turned away. Life really wasn't fair.

After a long silence passed between them, Jerry said, "Granny Peg hasn't heard any word from Boatswain. Miss Elizabeth wrote the man in Staunton, but she hasn't had an answer."

Paxton had told Sam that Ma had made the Major promise not to send Boatswain to Richmond, to sell him to a family in the neighborhood. That way, he could visit Granny Peg and his children, Jerry and Lucy. But the Major had probably broken his word. Instances like that tempted Sam to tell Jerry they were kin. But he stopped himself. No good would come of Jerry knowing a thing like that.

"Granny Peg thinks the Major sold Boatswain cause he didn't like being shown up all the time," Jerry said.

That surprised Sam. He'd never considered his father sold Boatswain for any reason other than money. Could Granny Peg be right? Boatswain knew more about farming and tending livestock than anybody else, but the Major didn't listen to him, either. The sunlight cut through the tree canopy, and a mellow wind passed over, warm yet crisp with the feel of autumn. Sam splashed Jerry again, this time with a handful of water. Jerry immediately responded in kind, and soon, they were throwing buckets of water at each other, laughing and shouting.

That spooked the big mare, and Jerry ran to retrieve her. Sam collected the other horses. Cousin Matthew's pants were wet and covered in sand and mud beneath the knees. Cousin Patsy would forgive him, but he'd have to make a good show of his remorse. He almost looked forward to it, for that would give him extra time with her.

Jerry walked ahead, leaving Sam to wonder about the world and his place in it. Then his stomach began to grumble. He cut ahead of Jerry and went through a field gone fallow with tall grass. His pants legs picked up dozens of cockleburs. Those, he would have to remove himself. Maybe he was a hopeless cause, like people said— reckless, careless, thoughtless. He didn't do it on purpose, though.

"Sam!" came a call. "Wait up." Paxton ran toward him.

"Hey, you're not going to believe what I just heard," Paxton said when he caught up with Sam. "The boys from Tory Hollow are planning to join up with Aaron Burr." Paxton's eyes were as vibrant as ever.

Sam asked with some hesitancy, "Are you planning on going with them?"

"Heck yeah. They say Burr is going all the way to Tejas to start a new country."

"When are you leaving?"

"Just as soon as we find you a decent gun. As big as you are, you'll pass for sixteen."

Sam's heart leapt, and the sullenness evaporated as though the sun had poked through the clouds and shone a bright new light on his future.

"You want me to come?"

The bay tugged on the lead, straining to graze farther away.

"Of course. This is what we've been waiting for."

"I'm supposed to have John's musket when he gets his new rifle next month." Sam's pulse quickened at the thought they would be leaving soon.

"That's what I'm thinking. We could leave right after. They're calling men to muster at Blennerhassett Island."

"Where's that?"

"Somewhere on the Ohio."

They resumed walking, and Sam had to pull hard to get the horses to stop feeding.

"But we have to keep quiet about it," Paxton said.

"What about Robert?"

"He's not coming. Everyone is going to be surprised."

Sam laughed. "And jealous. John will turn green with envy, won't he?"

"The Major will be furious, but we'll be long gone by then."

The happiness was almost unbearable, so full did Sam feel at the moment. And he didn't know how to keep a secret of such magnitude. A pang of remorse gripped him suddenly. What about Ma? Only moments before, he'd been mad at her for scolding him about the pants. The idea of leaving her brought a deep sadness to his heart, but after a moment, Sam soothed his conscience when he imagined coming home after a long while with riches enough to make his mother's life a comfort. He could feel her pride in him, which revived his determination to join his brother.

Paxton kept his voice low as they approached their wagons. "With Burr, we will find our fame and fortune."

Sam stopped, not wanting to end the conversation. "What's 'fame' mean, exactly?"

"It's when the whole world knows your name."

"That's what I want," Sam said.

"You do have a big head." Paxton grabbed Sam by the nape of the neck and gave him a gentle squeeze, then he slung an arm around Sam's shoulder and laughed. "I'll take the fortune and leave all the fame to you, brother."

Chapter Three

The new year came around, and Sam received John's old musket. His brother had not properly cared for the gun. Sam spent hours cleaning out the fouling, unsure if the gun would fire properly. The thought of joining Burr's army kept him at the task.

Then news came that President Jefferson had issued a warrant for Aaron Burr's arrest. The very next day, a fearsome nor'easter blew icy rain and sleet for two days, the worst storm Sam could remember. Everyone stayed indoors except for trips to the privy and tending the animals. The morning the storm broke, Paxton woke with a high fever and a rash on his chest, a definite sign of the scarlet fever. Ma had Granny Peg set up a bed in the front parlor. Only Granny Peg and Ma went near Paxton.

As a light snow fell steadily outside, Sam spent the long, idle hours poring over the Morse geography book, sitting at a window where the light was dim but serviceable. He traced his finger along the Ohio River where it poured into the Mississippi. Visions of running off with Paxton turned over in his mind constantly, shaping and reforming into ever grander adventures, although now, Sam sensed uncertainty about Burr's future and worried about Paxton's speedy recovery.

Winter finally softened with the blessing of a late-January thaw. They would pay for the reprieve with ice and snow again before spring arrived, but for the time being, the world outside came alive under the newfound warmth of a nearly forgotten sun. The Major left for an inspection tour on the other side of the Alleghenies. He threatened it would be his last with the militia, but he'd been saying that for months.

The next day, Ma sent Robert and James into town for salt, sugar, flour, and whatever meat they could find. Sam was sitting in the keeping room and reading when his mother came to him. John walked in behind her.

"John is going hunting today," she said. "I want you to go with him."

"Can't I go on my own or take Jerry with me?"

"Jerry's got work here," she said.

John poked Sam on one shoulder. "Forsake not your mother's teaching, young fool." Then he left the room.

Sam resented that he was expected to respect John's place in the family yet stay silent about his brother's shortcomings. Whenever Sam pointed out John's faults, he was punished or berated by their father.

"But, Ma, aren't you afraid John might accidentally shoot me? You know how bad an aim he is." Sam turned his face to his mother, trying to look earnest.

Granny Peg laughed. "He thinks those big blue eyes of his can charm a turtle from its shell."

"I don't have time to argue with you, Sam." Ma gave Granny Peg a stern frown.

"Why can't William do it?"

"I sent William to Mr. Trimble's to borrow some eggs."

Half their chickens had died from the severe cold, and for days, not one hen could be spared for the table.

Sam pulled on a jacket and threw a wool blanket around his shoulders. He took the old musket and met John outside. His brother held the new single-bore long rifle he'd been given on his twenty-first birthday. John also carried the powder horn and the waist pouch with the shot balls and the small patches of cloth needed to load the gun.

Sam wondered if the musket would fare better than his old gun, a fowling piece that could barely knock a pigeon from a tree. Muskets, with their smoothbore barrels, were notorious for having erratic trajectories. And Sam had had no time to discover the uniqueness of John's old gun, to remove any rust in the barrel, or find any other deficiencies caused by his brother's poor maintenance.

The ice clinging to the roofline dripped loudly onto the soggy ground. Sam turned his face toward the sun and breathed in the warm, clean air. He sprinted ahead of John then waited at the edge of the woods. When John caught up, Sam took the powder horn from him and a ball from the pouch then poured a little bit of the black powder into the pan on the musket. He closed the frizzen and lowered the stock, pointing the barrel up to pour powder into the muzzle. Sam carefully wrapped a ball with a small cloth patch then pressed the ball inside. He finished the job by using the ramrod to push the shot ball all the way down to the bottom of the barrel.

"You go ahead," Sam said. "You're so clumsy you might trip and shoot me in the back."

"You're going to hell one day."

"If you're not there, it'll be heaven for me."

John huffed off in the direction of Prospect Hill. Sam followed at a distance, not wanting to be any closer than needed, because forgetting about his tiresome brother was easier when surrounded by the majesty of the forest.

A thick bed of leaf mold covered the ground. Icicles clung to the bare limbs, glistening in the sunshine. A hawk screeched, and smaller birds chattered. Every so often, a shard of ice would lose its grip and shatter on the ground. Sam saw a squirrel scampering up a tree. He thought about trying to shoot it. Unsure of the musket, he waited for a bigger target before testing the aim. His eyes scoured the forest floor, looking for the neat piles of bean-sized pellets that meant deer were in the area.

They crossed Sheep Creek by leaping over some large slate boulders. Then they skirted Mr. Alexander's apple orchard, now a tangle of bleak, leafless limbs. An old trace cut along the eastern slope of Prospect Hill, through a thick stand of sumac trees. After wandering through the woods, they went down to the South River for water. There, Sam remembered a salt lick on the other side of Adams Peak. They were several miles from Timber Ridge.

"We'll miss dinner," John said.

"You can go back if you want," Sam said. "But leave me the rifle."

John didn't take the bait, so they doubled back to cross the footbridge above Falling Run and turned up the trail leading through

Dismal Hollow, then they cut along the tree line north of Adams Peak. Sam took the lead, descending the ravine that ended at the duck pond on Irish Creek, in a place called the Punchbowl, where a large salt lick lay near a spring.

Sure enough, a young buck had its forelegs spread wide to lick the minerals off the rock. Sam and John stayed under the cover of some maple trees, about fifteen yards away. John hesitated. The deer lifted his head, sniffing the air. The wind had shifted, and Sam knew the animal was on to them. John took aim and pulled the trigger, but the deer was already in motion when the ball struck. The animal bounded away, up into the hills.

"We've lost him," John said. "We'll not catch him now."

"He's wounded. We have to kill him."

John looked up at the sky. "It's already late."

"Go home if you must, but I'm going to find him before the wolves do." Sam grabbed the rifle from John and reloaded it.

"Give it back," John said.

"No, you had your chance." Sam thrust the old musket at John.

With the rifle in hand, Sam moved on, looking for the trail of blood. John would follow, not out of a sense of righteousness but because his brother wouldn't want all the credit for the kill to go to Sam.

Sam quickly picked up the deer's trail. At times, the young buck would stop to rest then bolt when Sam came close. He followed the deer for over a mile up and down Whetstone Ridge, each time getting a little nearer before the deer would sprint away. Sam lost the animal around the spot where Big Bend Creek flowed into the Irish. He stopped and listened, his eyes scanning the heavy woodland. Then, about thirty feet away, he spied the deer lying in the brush. The young buck turned its head. Sam took quick aim and fired.

John reached the kill first. Sam's shot had landed clean between the eyes. Using their knives, they gutted and dressed the small buck, bleeding it out as much as possible before Sam hoisted the carcass across his shoulders. It was heavy yet gave off a pleasant warmth. They started for home. John carried both the rifle and the musket and walked ahead. Sam didn't bother to keep up. The quiet of the woods and the satisfaction of the meat he would contribute to the family table kept him in good spirits.

He carefully crossed Sheep Creek, his strength waning as he climbed the rise on the other side. When he reached the top, the barren apple trees were in the shadows of the western light.

John waited for him. Sam took a moment to catch his breath.

"You're tired. Give it to me," John said.

"No. It's mine."

"I shot him first," John proclaimed.

"It's the kill that counts," Sam said. "Besides, you were going to leave the wolves to finish the job."

"It is your duty to me! The Apostle Peter preached, 'Ye who are younger, obey your elders.'"

"I don't need your Bible verses." Sam started to walk on, slowly.

"You shouldn't defy your betters."

Then Sam stopped and set the buck on the ground. "Betters!" he cried out. "You don't care for your tools, you're untidy, and you blame me for your own mistakes. Jerry would have been more help than you today."

"Who are you to judge me? You're just an ignorant, lazy boy and a slave lover."

"Ignorant? You're the chucklehead. You and James are too meek to venture out on your own. Paxton and I are leaving soon. We'll not hang on to the hind teat forever."

John's face went through a series of contortions as his mind appeared to wrestle meaning from Sam's words. "Good riddance." He stomped off, leaving Sam with the carcass.

Sam lingered a while to regain his strength. The time, though, brought only self-recrimination. He didn't know why he let John provoke him. He'd promised Paxton to keep their plans a secret. The last quarter mile, he walked slowly, wracked with guilt. He knew he would get a beating from his father, yet disappointing Paxton weighed more heavily than the buck on his shoulders.

As their barn came into view, Sam saw his father's sorrel mare in the paddock, the saddle still on. An unfamiliar horse was hitched nearby. Sam walked to the kitchen, bending down to enter with the carcass still on his shoulders.

Granny Peg was tending the fire as Lucy churned butter and Isabella sat on the floor, wrapped in a blanket.

Sam straightened up. "Look what I brought, Granny Peg." At least he could enjoy someone's approval.

She turned to him. "Take it outside. Go to your mother. Miss Elizabeth needs her children now."

Sam didn't understand. "Don't you want me to string it up for you?"

Granny Peg stoked the gray coals, sending sparks flying around the large iron pot hanging in the hearth. "No, leave it by the door."

He dropped the carcass on the ground just outside the kitchen. Then he went back and stood in the doorway.

"Granny Peg, what's wrong?"

She lifted her eyes to Sam. "Your pa's dead."

A hard freeze descended, and the Major's body didn't reach Timber Ridge for two days. The driver brought a bill from Callaghan's Tavern for room and board and the use of the wagon.

Ma glanced down at the paper and handed it over to James.

"The kitchen's out back," she told the driver. "After you bring my husband inside, my servant will have something for you."

Ma turned to the others, saying, "John and Robert, help this man get your father into the parlor. Sam, go fetch Mrs. Lyle's woman. Peggy will need the help."

Sam ran down the south side of Maple Hill and to the back door of Daniel Lyle's house. After he delivered the message to a servant, he set off for the woods. Shocked by the news of his father's death, Sam couldn't help but feel a certain relief, knowing the fight with John while they'd been hunting would be forgotten. His father's death hadn't seemed real until Sam saw the body. He felt no sadness, just an emptiness he couldn't shake, and he didn't know if he and Paxton could leave their mother now. That didn't seem possible. But a part of him refused to give up their dream of venturing off on their own.

The sun fell below the tree line, casting long shadows by the time Sam returned home. He entered through the back door and was immediately greeted by the pungent smell of camphor. Polly and Eliza were in the keeping room. James sat at the Major's desk in the library, toiling over the account books under the light of a candle.

Sam moved cautiously into the hallway and peered into the parlor from afar. In the fading light, he saw his father's body stretched out on their dining table. The Major had been dressed in a heavy linen gown. His mother had her back to Sam as she bent over to snip off a thick strand of the Major's hair.

Mrs. Lyle's woman and Granny Peg passed him as they left the room.

The Lyle woman told Granny Peg, "You won't need no stones. This cold will keep him from puffing up."

Sam moved closer but didn't venture into the room. John sat in the corner, his shoulders slumped forward and his head buried in his chest. His mother lit a candle and turned to place it in the window. Quietly, Sam went to John. His brother didn't move.

Very gently, he placed his fingertips on John's shoulder and whispered, "I'm sorry."

Not even the slightest reaction came from John. The grief had carried his brother into a stupor. Strangely, Sam couldn't feel the same way about his father's death, yet he could relate to his brother's deep sorrow, knowing how horrible he would feel if Ma suddenly died.

The next morning, Tom's father, William Letcher, came to measure for a coffin.

In the days that followed, family and friends from the neighboring farms came to the house, carrying food and a morbid curiosity, and each day brought another bill from a tavern or an invoice from a tradesman. Almost overnight, deep lines appeared on Ma's forehead, and a look of stony resignation never left her face. Robert went to stay with Ma's family four miles away in Brownsburg, mostly to be near Martha McChesney. James did his chores and worked on the accounts. William avoided the front of the house. Sam did too. Paxton moved upstairs, no longer contagious yet still weak. Granny Peg kept Isabella with her in the kitchen and acted as though not much had happened except she was more solicitous of Ma. Only John stayed in the parlor, as though he was waiting for the Major to wake.

Word came that a burial plot had been dug in the cemetery at High Bridge Presbyterian Church.

"Why do we have to go all the way up the valley when there's a cemetery at Timber Ridge?" Sam asked.

Paxton sat up in bed, a wool shawl around his shoulders. "Ma said the Major wanted to be near his cousins."

"We have cousins here."

"It was the bad feelings over Ann Henderson."

High Bridge was twelve miles away, close to Cousin Matthew's house and the church where Reverend Houston was pastor. Sam thought about what he'd heard the Reverend Houston say about his father only a few months before. Sam hadn't told Paxton then, and he didn't say anything now. Instead, he wrestled alone with the shame of knowing his father had not been respected, not even by the servants. Sadly, the Major had held himself in a high opinion, but almost everyone else had judged him an incompetent fool. Sam now understood why people would claim "ignorance is bliss."

The day the coffin arrived, Ma had Sam and Jerry fit their new five-horse wagon with the cloth covering. Early the next morning, with the Major's body secure in a plain pine box and lying on the bed of the buckboard, James took the reins with Ma beside him. Robert rode his own horse, and John sat atop the Major's sorrel mare. Sam drove the large covered wagon. It was meant for hauling heavy goods, so it had no bench seat, and he walked on the left side, just behind the team of horses. At the back, William rode the lazy board to work the brake if needed.

Ma insisted Paxton travel under cover in the wagon with the two girls and Granny Peg. Isabella had been left at home with Lucy and Jerry. The family made the journey up the valley under a sky of dusky, low-hanging clouds that threatened snow. When they arrived at High Bridge Church, the Houston and Paxton clans were gathered outside. The Major's married sisters and their husbands—Letcher, McKee, McClung, and Hopkins—were there. Sam didn't see any of the cousins near his age.

Slowly, Sam and his brothers carried the coffin behind the church and down the eastern slope.

When they started to set it down on top of the ropes laid out next to the deep pit, Ma cried out, "No! Turn it around. His feet need to be toward the east so he can rise up facing the Lord on the Day of Resurrection."

After turning the coffin as his mother wanted, Sam and his

brothers moved to stand near her. Reverend Houston clutched a large Bible close to his chest as he spoke over a steady wind.

"There are those around us who believe a man should eat and drink merrily, for tomorrow we will die. Do not be deceived by this false thinking. Evil company corrupts good morals. Come to a sober and right mind, and sin no more. For those who lack the knowledge of God, I say this to your shame."

A raven cawed loudly from a leafless poplar at the edge of the cemetery. The Reverend Houston paused, lowering his head while he lifted the Bible up with outstretched arms. Sam looked around. His mother had her lips pressed together. James was looking down at the ground with little emotion on his face. Tears rolled freely down John's cheeks. Paxton appeared pale, standing next to Robert, and Robert, the brother who most resembled their father with his stiff bearing and handsome face, seemed already removed from the family.

The reverend's voice boomed out again. "Only God knows what death holds for us."

The sun appeared through a break in the clouds, and a ray of light quickly swept over the coffin. Then the grayness returned.

The reverend nodded, and Sam, James, John, and Robert each took one of the ropes. The mourners stepped back, allowing the brothers to lift the coffin and lower it slowly and steadily. It was nearly to the bottom when John yelped and the rope slipped through his hands. The coffin landed awkwardly, giving off a loud plunk against the cold, dark earth. No one said a word while John stood crying uncontrollably. Sam thought someone should go and comfort John, but no one moved. The entire family stood like the tombstones, unflinching weathered testaments to the harshness of life.

The reverend bent his head again and called out over John's sobs, "Now, let us pray for Samuel Davidson Houston's soul. Jesus died for our sins so that those who hold their faith may rise again. All others will have lived in vain. For the wages of sin is eternal death, and our cousin surely needs our prayers now and forever. Amen."

A gasp escaped from Ma, and she turned and moved away from the grave. Granny Peg followed her, and Eliza trailed behind them. Polly clung to Sam, and he hugged her tightly. John had stopped weeping and glared at the reverend with angry water in his eyes.

Cousin Matthew grabbed a fistful of dirt and dropped it into the grave. Each of the male relatives did the same, then the mourning party began to drift away, leaving the gravediggers to finish the work. In a long, slow, quiet procession, the mourners walked the quarter mile to Cousin Matthew's home. The family wagons had already been driven over by servants.

Cousin Matthew had a new two-story red brick house, much finer than the house at Timber Ridge. On the first floor, Matthew Houston ran a general store and a tavern. A grand feast greeted the funeral party in the large hall. Cousin Patsy was moving about the room. Sam wished he could talk to her, but she was busy with the guests. Most of the men, including Reverend Houston, escaped into the tavern room, where Cousin Matthew poured cider from a large barrel. The other women surrounded his mother.

Sam wandered into the general store. The shelves were full of staples—flour, sugar, dried fruits, and bolts of calico. Other fancy items he didn't recognize were there also.

Robert was in the tavern with their Paxton cousins from Brownsburg.

Sam filled a plate with food but, for once, had little appetite.

Just as he was joining the other brothers outside on the back porch, John said, "The gall to give Ma a bill for the gravediggers today."

"It's better than waiting a month," James said.

"He shouldn't have said what he did." John rubbed his nose with his sleeve.

"Who shouldn't have said what?" Sam asked.

"The reverend shouldn't have said the Major was a sinner and a drinker!" John groused.

Paxton sat leaning against a column. "We're all sinners." His voice was weak.

"The invoices prove the Major drank spirits," James said.

John's face went red. "We shouldn't pay any of them. They're lies."

"They can't all be lies," James replied. "But likely, the sums have been exaggerated since the Major's not here to question them."

Paxton lifted his head, his eyes bright with anger. "The Major has left us without a penny in the purse and squandered our inheritance."

John snarled at Paxton. "Don't ever say that about our father again."

"I am only saying what everybody knows is true." Paxton turned his eyes away.

John lunged at Paxton and began to kick him. From a seated position, Paxton couldn't fight back easily, and he didn't appear to have the strength to get quickly to his feet, so Sam leapt to his brother's aid. He grabbed John around the waist and wrestled him off the porch. Sam jumped down after him, swinging his arms at his brother, driven by a pleasure he couldn't control. John hit back, but Sam had become as tall and big as his brother. Sam threw a fist and caught John on the chin with a loud smack.

James got between them.

"You are a devil," John sputtered between ragged breaths. "You're the reason our father died too early. Your laziness and insolence caused me to lose my father."

Startled by the depth of John's malice, Sam stood silent, regretting the sympathy he'd felt for his brother only a few moments ago at the gravesite.

Ma appeared on the porch with some of the other family members. Sam looked for Paxton, but his brother must have gone inside. Sam's hand was aching, and he stalked away. He walked down to the fence enclosing a pasture of cattle and sheep. Despite the cold, he stayed there brooding, too angry to think, unwilling to face his mother.

Sam waited until he saw their wagons hitched and ready to leave. He wished he'd eaten more. He thought about the shelves in Cousin Matthew's store, full of expensive goods his own family could never afford to buy. He considered the free-flowing cider in the tavern and didn't know what to think. He felt like an outsider, caught between what people said about piety and goodness and the evidence of a different world, one full of sinners.

Two days later, Mr. Kinneer and Duncan Campbell came to the house after the dinner hour. Ma gathered the family in the front parlor. Sam stood behind Paxton, who sat next to Polly. Without any explanation, Mr. Campbell began to read aloud from a sheaf of papers.

"In the name of God Amen, I, Samuel Houston of Timber Ridge, Rockbridge County, and the State of Virginia frame this instrument with my own hand and do constitute it my last will and testament."

He stopped and cleared his throat.

Polly cried. Sam put a hand on her trembling shoulder.

Mr. Campbell read on: "Item: I order that my funeral charges and all my just debt be punctually paid by my executors."

Sam asked, "What's an executor?"

Ma turned her head slightly, enough for Sam to know he needed to stay quiet.

Mr. Campbell continued, "Item: I give and bequeath my beloved wife, Elizabeth, all my household furniture together with the kitchen and all implements of husbandry and all my stock of cattle, sheep, and hogs and also all my horse creatures except two, which I give and bequeath unto my son John a dark bay which is called his and a sorrel which I generally ride."

Sam looked out the window at the gravestones in the cemetery behind the Old Stone Church. A light drizzle was falling, and he watched a line of robins work their way through the grass.

"She is also to give my sons Paxton, Samuel, and William, and my daughters Isabella, Polly, and Eliza each a good horse and saddle when they may actually need them..."

Why don't James or Robert receive a horse, while John gets two? That didn't seem fair. Sam glanced over at his brothers. Robert stood rigid with no expression, and James leaned forward in his chair with his elbows on his knees, head down.

"My executors..." Mr. Campbell said.

Campbell's voice droned on, but Sam was only half listening when it came to the technical words.

"Out of said moneys to enable them to move with convenience as they may find it most eligible to some new country..."

New country? What about Timber Ridge? Who will inherit the farm? Sam had thought for sure it would be John.

Then Mr. Campbell droned on about things that didn't mean anything until Sam heard the words "purchase lands" followed by "at the decease of my wife."

A shudder of desolation cut through to Sam's very core, and in a panic, he darted his eyes to Ma. His mother was sitting as she always did, hands in her lap, her head held high and her shoulders squared. Seeing her relieved the anxiety.

"In the following manner, to my son John, two shares and to all my other children, one share each..."

Sam shook his head and let out a sigh. In both life and death, the Major had made sure everyone knew he favored his second son above all others.

"During her widowhood, my wife is to also retain her saddle and my bridle. She is also to have the disposal of my books..."

At least John wouldn't get all the books. He never read anything but the Bible anyway.

"To my son John, my sword, if it is not disposed of in my lifetime, and my apparel. In consequence of my son John receiving the greatest dividend, he is to pay strict attention to my family and endeavor to see them raised and treated with justice."

Sam scoffed out loud and received another warning eye from his mother.

"My executors are the guardians of my children until they shall arrive at the lawful age, and I would recommend that they put my sons to such trades as may be most beneficial."

A trade? What kind of trade?

"And I do appoint as executors of this, my last will and testament, my wife Elizabeth..."

Thank goodness for that.

"And my sons James Houston and John Houston."

Immediately, Sam turned toward John. A sly smile crossed his brother's lips. Sam's throat went dry, and his lips stuck together. He could barely breathe throughout the rest of the reading.

When it finally ceased, he blurted, "Why does Isabella get a horse but Robert doesn't?"

"Sam!" his mother said. "Your father did as he thought best. Now either stay quiet or leave the room."

Sam's face grew hot, and everyone lowered their heads except John, who smiled at Sam with that evil grin. He didn't know why he had ever wasted his sympathy on John. Sam gripped the back of

Paxton's chair as the horror of being under John's thumb sank in.

Mr. Kinneer stood to address the family. Rubbing his hands together, he said, "The Major and Mrs. Houston sold Timber Ridge to me last September."

Timber Ridge is gone? Sam wondered who else had known. Only William looked surprised.

That must have been why the Major bought the five-horse wagon. Then all the signs fell into place—the animosity with the Lyles over Ann Henderson, the failing farm, the threats to quit the militia—everything had been in plain sight, but Sam had been blinded by his own dreams. Surely, that explained why Ma had been so impatient and stern those past months. How his mother must have suffered! Sam imagined the comedown she must have been feeling, and the heat rose again, fueled by thoughts of the embarrassing things the neighbors would say behind her back, how the proud Elizabeth Blair Paxton Houston had lost her home because her husband squandered it away. The shame brought tears to his eyes, and his heart wept quietly for his mother's pride.

After Mr. Kinneer and Mr. Campbell left, Paxton and Sam went outside alone.

"Did you know?"

Paxton nodded. "I couldn't tell you. I promised Mr. Kinneer I wouldn't."

"Who else knew?"

"I'm not sure. Doesn't matter now." Paxton gave Sam a weak smile. "Looks like we're leaving after all. Just not the way we wanted."

Chapter Four

What furniture hadn't been sold or given away was stowed and wouldn't be unpacked until they reached Tennessee. By the light of candles, Sam and Jerry hitched up the five-horse wagon, positioning the mare Goose as the main wheeler. The dark bay had to be in the lead because he had a tendency to bite. James and Robert readied the buckboard wagon, where Granny Peg sat with Isabella atop the oiled wool tarps protecting their small luggage.

Dawn broke, and the morning light silvered the frost on the fields. Paxton climbed onto the lazy board. He'd regained some of his strength, but his vitality had not been fully restored. Standing at the side of the wagon, Sam flicked the reins. Foggy plumes of breath rose from the horses as they snorted and grunted. The dark bay strained against the holster, but the wagon didn't lurch forward until Goose decided to move, and thus they began the journey.

The buckboard followed with Ma and the two younger girls walking alongside. William held the lead on one milk cow, and Jerry walked with the other two cows in tow. In the rear position, John rode the Major's sorrel mare.

Sam had expected some momentous feeling to accompany their departure. But leaving Timber Ridge didn't seem out of the ordinary. He felt like they were simply taking a trip into town. After the initial shock of the Major's death, life had proceeded as usual. In a twist of fate, last year's spring planting had produced bounties of corn, wheat, and tobacco in the fall. Except for the occasional visit from Mr. Kinneer, Sam hadn't really believed they would be leaving. Only in early winter, when the livestock—pigs, sheep, and cattle—were sold or butchered did he begin to feel their move to Tennessee would really happen.

The horses trudged slowly under the heavy load. Late afternoon had come by the time they reached Cousin Matthew's place at Vine Oaks. Cousin Patsy had supper waiting for them. The family retired early, sleeping on straw mattresses placed in the hallway outside the tavern and the mercantile store. Jerry went to stay in the servants' quarters, but Granny Peg bedded down with the family so that Isabella could sleep beside her.

In the morning, Sam drove the large wagon a few miles to Cousin Matthew's mill on Cedar Creek. Ma was with him, and Jerry came too. Sam knew what was coming, and he tried to steel himself for the parting.

Cousin Matthew met them at the entrance. Over the door were the words *Laborare Est Orare* burned into a wooden board. Sam asked what it meant.

"Work is prayer," Cousin Matthew told him.

The mill workers were hauling out bags of feed.

Cousin Matthew turned to Ma. "I wrote to our kin in Botetourt. My cousin will be expecting you."

"Thank you. I sent word to my brother's daughter at Seven Mile Ford. If the Lord favors us with good weather, we may be able to make it without wasting money on lodging."

Ma then turned to Sam. "Take the crate of books from the wagon."

"Why?"

"It's too much weight."

"Oh, Ma," Sam groaned.

"Sam, we talked about this. There will be no time for books. You can keep the dictionary. The others are to be left with Cousin Matthew."

"But I need something to read when we get to Tennessee!"

His mother sighed. "One extra book. That's all."

"Why are you giving away everything I love?"

"Sam," his mother said sternly, "we talked about all this. Everyone has to make sacrifices."

Sam caught Cousin Matthew's eye but found no sympathy there.

"I have some business with Cousin Matthew to settle. By the time we're done, I expect the books to be removed and the feed to be stowed."

Ma went inside the mill house with Cousin Matthew.

Sam knew what the business was—had known for weeks—but it was still the one event Sam didn't want to believe would happen. In early January, Ma had asked Sam to drive her into town in the buckboard. Their first stop was to the cobbler's shop. When they went inside, to Sam's surprise, his mother unwrapped the bundle she was carrying and turned over her fine silver carving set to pay for new soles on the family's shoes. Their next stop was the county clerk's office, a small cabin behind the courthouse.

"Wait for me here," Ma said.

Not long thereafter, his mother returned with some papers in her hand.

"What's this for?" Sam asked.

"Mr. Reid made a copy of my father's will. I can't risk taking Peggy to Tennessee if I don't have proof she belongs to us. Someone might try to steal her from me."

"What about Jerry and Lucy and the boys?"

"We can't take Lucy and her babies."

"Why not?"

"I can't afford to feed them. Lucy and her children will be better off with Aunt Bettie."

"But Jerry's coming with us, isn't he?"

"Cousin Matthew is going to take Jerry to work in his mill."

Sam had sat silent for a while, for it had never occurred to him that Jerry wouldn't be with him always.

"Peggy knows about Lucy, but I haven't told her about Jerry—not yet. I'm telling you now so that you can prepare yourself. I know how fond of Jerry you are."

At the time, Sam had put it out of his mind, but now, he sighed loudly, wondering if Jerry knew he'd be staying with Cousin Matthew. Together, they lifted the crate from the wagon and placed it on the ground. Sam picked up the geography book. *Too large.* He searched for something he could carry in his knapsack and discovered a small but thick volume. *The Iliad* fit his palm easily, and he hoped it would offer hours of reading.

Ma and Cousin Matthew came out a little later. His mother called to Jerry, who dutifully walked over. Sam's nose tingled, and his eyes began to water. He clenched his teeth when Cousin Matthew approached Jerry.

"You're going to work in the mill," his cousin said. "It's a good trade."

Jerry nodded.

Sam had to turn away as a terrible sadness welled up in his chest, making breathing hard. He went to the front of the wagon, and without another word to his friend, Sam took hold of the reins. His mother joined him. As Sam drove the wagon away from the mill, a bundle of unsettling feelings came upon him. He should've been the one to stay with Cousin Matthew. He'd always looked up to his cousin and held a special fondness for Patsy. They were the prosperous ones in the extended Houston clan. A strange sort of resentment bubbled up, and for an instant, Sam wished he could trade places with Jerry. But he knew deep down that "Work Is Prayer" was not a motto he could heed. Jerry was better suited to work with Cousin Matthew, for he was reliable and worked hard without complaint. The sense of envy lingered until Sam and his mother met the rest of the family at the High Bridge cemetery. Ma walked straight to Granny Peg.

"Did he complain or cry?" Granny Peg asked, her eyes full of tears.

"He was a good boy. Cousin Matthew is pleased to have him. He'll take good care of Jerry."

Then Ma led the family behind the church. The mound over their father's grave had settled. A small gray fieldstone with one word, "Houston," lay plain and simple in the ground. How pitiful the gravestone was, compared to the others in the cemetery. How pathetic that the family had been brought so low that they couldn't afford to have his father's full name chiseled on the marker. The shame of it settled in Sam's chest. *How long have we been the poor relations in the family?* He was suddenly glad they were leaving Virginia and all the reminders of his father's failure.

After a short prayer, the small caravan moved off toward the Great Wagon Road. It would take Sam farther south than he'd ever been. Yet the country looked the same, farms nestled in the valleys and heavily wooded hills with a creek or stream to ford every few miles.

By midday, Sam felt the road descending into the James River Valley. The path led them to a wide expanse of rocky shoals shallow enough to ford the river.

As they waited at the crossing, a man told Sam, "Don't feed your horses now. Only give 'em water so they'll hurry on. That way, they learn what's waiting for them on the other side."

The buckboard wagon went first, with Ma and the two girls joining Granny Peg and Isabella atop the baggage. William tethered the cow to the back of Sam's wagon before climbing up behind John on the sorrel mare. Paxton stayed on the lazy board, and Sam mounted Goose, looping the long reins in both hands. He urged the horses into the water, offering enough lead to let them carefully pick their way over the rocky riverbed.

Once safely across, the horses were fed while James and Robert checked both wagons for damage. An hour before sunset, they stopped along Mill Creek, where another Houston cousin had a farm.

With the horses tended to and safe in the paddock for the night, the brothers joined the family for a thin stew of pork and winter squash. Ma and the two younger girls slept in the house while the brothers bunked in the barn. They made a bed for Granny Peg and Isabella among the bales of hay because his poor sister would cry if she was separated from Granny Peg.

The next day, the caravan moved on. The sun shone, but a boisterous wind whipped up the dust on the road. Each time after they crossed a creek or stream, Goose would shake her head and snort, refusing to budge until Sam gave her a handful of oats.

Life on the road fell into a routine. An hour or so before sunset, they would find a place to camp; unhitch the wagon; water, feed, and brush the horses; then tie them up for the night. The brothers took turns greasing the wheels and applying tar on the underside seams to keep the water from leaking through. Paxton did what he could, and John mostly lorded over everyone as though he wore a crown. After a meal of dried meat and cold biscuits, the family bedded down under the wagons, pressed against each other for warmth.

Their progress stalled as they neared Big Lick, where the trail to North Carolina forked off to the southeast. Sam climbed atop Goose to get a view of what lay ahead. The lanes narrowed between the buildings in town. A great shoving and pushing clogged the road as the travelers trying to turn onto the southeast road had to cut among the long wagon trains heading north. He supposed the wagons were going to the markets in Baltimore or Philadelphia.

Soon, a long line of black men chained together with iron collars came from the southeast path. Sam knew large plantations with hundreds of slaves existed in the Tidewater, but he'd never seen anything like this before. In Timber Ridge, most families owned no more than a dozen slaves. Sam watched what seemed an endless train of men tethered closely together, forced to move with a shuffling gait and their heads down, eyes fixed to the ground and shoulders slumped in resignation.

The white men who guarded the slaves carried whips. Suddenly, Sam's heart shuddered when he realized this might have been how Boatswain was treated if that man in Staunton had sold him to someone else. His stomach lurched into his throat. If the Major had lived, maybe he would have sent Jerry to the slave market in Richmond, where he would have been treated worse than the cattle and sheep being driven to market. At least the animals had no chains around their necks.

Sam turned away, breathing deeply, trying to settle his feelings. His mother had made sure Jerry would be safe with Cousin Matthew. He said a small prayer, asking God to take care of Boatswain, too, wherever he might have been. Then he had another terrible thought. *Is Granny Peg thinking the same thing?* Surely, this spectacle of life's injustice would be worse for her. She must be worried for Boatswain and her children but helpless to do anything about it.

After an hour of waiting, their caravan passed through Big Lick. That afternoon, they stopped to camp at a sandy beach on the Staunton River. Once the horses were settled, Sam went out to the banks of the river, hoping to find comfort in the soft, murmuring waters. The sun dipped below the horizon, and a slender crescent moon appeared in the western sky.

Sam wished he'd smiled at Jerry or at least nodded one last time, to acknowledge the times they'd wandered through hollows and hills, not as master and slave but as friends and companions. Had Jerry known he was Sam's favorite person to be around, especially when Sam wanted company without an intruding conversation? He already missed Jerry's warm, generous dark eyes and his easygoing nature and worried that he might never see his friend again.

Then, out of the blue, Sam realized that after he found his fame and fortune, he could return to Cousin Matthew's and buy Jerry's freedom. That eased Sam's mind, and he lay back and looked up at the stars twinkling in the darkening sky. How much time had passed since they left Timber Ridge? He counted from the twenty-third and realized what day it was: March second, his birthday.

He was fifteen years old, and for the first time, Sam felt nostalgic and sentimental about the past. The feelings came with a certain remorse for not having appreciated what he'd had when he was younger. *Is this how growing up works? Will every important milestone always be paired with losing something in the bargain?*

The next morning, the caravan plodded slowly for several miles across a sandy bottomland. Late in the afternoon, with their camp made, Sam climbed up a hill and sat on an outcropping overlooking the land below. With the skies clear in the west, he could see for miles. Low-ranging hills spread like ripples in a pond. A river meandered leisurely through a wide valley, forming double horseshoe bends with orchards and fields and pastures along the banks. Somewhere out there, he would find his destiny. A surge of confidence lifted his spirits, washing away any uncertainty about when or how Sam would make a name for himself.

At Dunkard's Bottom, his mother parted with a dollar and three cents for each wagon to cross the New River on Ingle's Ferry. The travel seemed to revive Paxton's energy. He and William traded places—William on the lazy board and Paxton with the milk cow, walking beside Sam.

"I'll be right as rain by the time we reach Tennessee. You'll see, Sam. As soon as the farm is established, we'll be off. I'll have a big, prosperous plantation, and you can do whatever you like."

Sam was heartened to hear Paxton talk with such confidence about the future. For hours, they speculated on where to go—the Mississippi Territory, Tejas, or maybe all the way past the Rockies like Lewis and Clark did.

The caravan made good progress under a string of mild late-winter days and a mellow westerly breeze, passing homesteads and barns and villages that seemed to blur together. When the road was level and well packed, Sam tethered the milk cow to the wagon, and William would ride the lazy board while Sam and Paxton sat atop the wheelers. From that vantage, Sam could observe the people in their doorways or behind fences. Until recently, he had been the one watching from the front stoop at Timber Ridge, staring and judging the passersby without even realizing it. Now, he was being observed and graded by strangers. That didn't feel altogether right, but it didn't feel wrong, either.

At night, the somnolent tumble of the wagon wheels seemed to lull Sam to sleep as though he never stopped moving. Undoing the hitch at the end of the day only to redo it again in the morning became drudgery, and he missed reading, yet the constant state of motion relieved the tedium he'd often felt at Timber Ridge. And apart from the times he cared for the animals, Sam didn't have to come in contact with his guardians, John and James, on most days, another unexpected benefit of traveling.

At Seven Mile Ford, the caravan took a turnoff to reach the farm where Ma's niece, Mary Edmondston, lived with her husband's family. A quarter mile along, the track opened into a pasture with milk cows and sheep. Smoke rising from a chimney promised a hot meal and a warm place to sleep. Thoughts of fresh bread and eggs frying in a skillet filled his head—anything would be better than hardtack and cold biscuits.

The house was stout and sturdy, smaller than the barn. Both had wide, steep-pitched roofs. A woman stood in the yard, wearing a peculiar white cap, unlike the box-shaped caps Ma sometimes wore. This one had a pointed end at the crown and side flaps that turned up like wings. The woman went quickly into the barn.

A man came out, followed by two women. Both wore aprons and the strange caps. Maybe one of them was Ma's niece.

"Mrs. Houston," the man said. "I'm Mary's husband, Charles Edmondston. Mary's inside with Oma." He turned toward the women in the caps. "These are my aunts, Bernadine and Girt."

Sam couldn't tell how old they were exactly because those strange caps hid their faces.

Ma and Granny Peg unloaded the blankets from the buckboard.

Charles carried the bulk of the items into the house. The taller aunt, Girt, stood ready to take the horses as Sam and William unhitched the wagon. Bernadine did the same for the buckboard.

Then Charles came back outside to spread hay for the animals along the fence. John unsaddled his horse, and Paxton took the cow to water. Once the animals were tended to, Sam and his brothers walked to the house. The windows had shutters decorated with six-point star cutouts and painted with flowers and trees. Inside was warm and pleasant. From a large hearth came the heavenly aroma of yeasty bread.

Ma, Granny Peg, and Sam's three sisters were seated on a bench at the table. Spread before them were bowls of potted cheese, hard-boiled eggs swimming with beets and onions, cold potatoes, and sour cabbage. A stack of plump sausages lay next to a haunch of ham. Sam swallowed hard at seeing a meal better than what Cousin Patsy had served them at Vine Oaks.

"Wash in the basin before you come to table."

Sam hadn't noticed the older woman in a high-backed chair. The cap she wore had the highest peak of all but no flaps to hide her face. Abundant white hair tried to escape from the sides. Her gray eyes were hard and commanding. As the brothers lined up at a cupboard where a wooden bowl held water to rinse their hands and faces, Sam surveyed the room. A staircase hid a bed in the nook beneath it. A baby slept in a wooden rocker not far from a young woman at the hearth. She, too, wore a cap but without the flaps.

Two benches sat at the table with a few stools. Oma, as the old woman was called, sat at the head of the table in the only chair in the room.

Sam rinsed in the basin. The cloth used to dry his hands and face was stitched with blue and pink flowers.

"Freshen the water, Bernadine," Oma said.

Bernadine took the basin in her red, coarse hands. Sam moved ahead of her and opened the door.

"Girt, redd up the room for Mrs. Houston and her girls."

"I can have my Peggy do that," Ma offered politely.

"No. Girt knows how to make the arrangements," Oma said.

Girt counted out four blankets and took them upstairs.

Sam looked at Oma, whose hands were soft and plump and white.

"My Charles made a good wife," Oma told Ma.

"Yes, my niece will be a dutiful wife, just like her own mother."

"Thankfully, she is good in the kitchen." Oma turned to Mary. "Bring the rolls out. Can't you smell they're about to burn, girl?"

Oma then looked at Ma and openly and freely said, "Girt's a doplic, too clumsy for the kitchen. Bernadine is rutschy, burning everything because she can never sit still."

No one said anything. Charles sat on a stool at the opposite end of the table from Oma. Mary set the pan of rolls near her husband. Steam rose from the hot rolls, and Sam wanted to grab one, but he knew that would not go unnoticed by the old woman, who ruled like a monarch from her throne. Sam stepped nearer the hearth, the biggest he'd ever seen.

Girt came down again and stood behind Oma's chair.

Bernadine brought in the basin of water.

Oma looked at Ma. "Have the daughters and your woman sit on the floor."

Ma told Granny Peg to take Isabella away from the table, and Polly and Eliza followed them.

"Take your seats," Oma told Sam and his brothers.

They slid onto the benches. Bernadine and her sister stood behind their mother while Mary stood behind Charles.

The old woman bowed her head, and Charles said the blessing in a language Sam didn't understand, although he heard a familiar pattern—*fodder, soh, un heilich geischt*—which he took for "Father, Son, and Holy Ghost."

"Bernadine, bring the honey," Oma commanded.

Bernadine moved to the cupboard and brought over a small wooden bowl then placed it near Oma.

"I refuse to buy sugar made from cane," the old woman said. "It is grown with slave labor in the most evil conditions."

Oma then nodded at Charles. "Carve the ham."

Sam took a hot roll and slathered it with apple butter. It was gone in two bites. Mary filled bowls with cabbage and potatoes and brought them to Granny Peg and the girls.

Oma told Ma, "Mary's mother writes that Mr. Houston left you with very little. Whatever you have, thank the Lord it's yours now. When Mr. Kirchner asked for my hand, my father refused to let me leave Pennsylvania without my own money. I've saved it for these two girls, for when they make a husband."

At that angle, Sam could see that Girt had a crooked eye and Bernadine a face like a bird's. They were older, not as old as Ma but older than Mary. Sadly, and without a doubt, these women would never make husbands as their mother wanted. Oma trained her eyes on Robert, the handsomest of the older brothers. Did she think she could tempt him to marry one of her daughters with the talk of money? James maybe, but Robert already had his heart set on Martha McChesney.

Oma directed her attention to Ma again, saying, "You'll be living near my daughter and her husband. I never would have let her leave if I knew the Tennesseans would go back on their word."

Confident that Oma had not deemed him old enough to be a husband for either of her daughters, and his tongue loosened by the warmth of the fire at his back and the thick slice of ham before him, Sam asked, "Back on their word about what?"

Those flinty gray eyes turned on him. Sam stopped chewing.

"Why, freeing the slaves. The Tennesseans abolished the immoral practice and then changed the laws to become a slave state."

Oma lowered her chin, facing Ma. "As it is my duty to share the plenty in my home with strangers, it is my duty to urge you to set your Negro woman free. I can send her to Pennsylvania, where she'll be safe with the Brethren."

The suddenness of Oma's offer to take Granny Peg startled Sam.

Granny Peg, wide-eyed and fearful, came to Ma's side. "Please, Miss Elizabeth, don't sell me."

Oma scoffed. "Why, I would not pay a penny. Mrs. Houston, you must free her of your own conscience. There will be no profit in it for you."

John cleared his throat loudly. "Saint Paul said, 'Servants, be obedient to your masters on this earth with fear and trembling, as unto Christ.'"

For once, John quoting the Bible came in handy and was a welcome retort to this haughty old woman trying to stir up trouble about Granny Peg.

As Oma leaned forward, about to lash her sharp tongue at John, Ma said, "I did not make the conditions we live with today. I thank you for your concern, but it would be cruel to thrust my Peggy among strangers, away from her family. As you can see, she is well cared for."

Oma grunted then tilted her head to one side. "Bernadine, stir the coals."

If only Sam could tell Oma that Granny Peg was likely kin to Mary. The old woman talked of freeing Granny Peg, but she treated her own daughters as though they were her slaves. Sadly, the sisters would not know freedom, not until their mother was dead and buried. No longer intimidated by the old woman, Sam reached for a second slice of ham.

When the meal was finished, Bernadine and Girt began to take away the platters and bowls.

When Ma rose to help them, Oma interceded, saying, "Mrs. Houston, take upstairs with your daughters and the Negro woman and ready for sleep. Mind you, make out the candle before you say your prayers."

Sam and his brothers laid their blankets on the floor around the hearth. Charles helped Oma from her chair and into a bed beneath the stairs. Sleep came quickly, and Sam didn't wake until he smelled bacon frying.

"It's making down outside," Oma said. "Mrs. Houston, you would be wise to wait."

A heavy drizzle was falling, but Ma was eager to leave. For hours, the wagons pushed against a heavy wind that carried a sharp bite, and everyone trudged through miles of muck and mud. When they reached Chilhowie, the sky was thick with dark-gray clouds, and the ground was too wet to sleep on. Ma paid two dollars and fifty cents for a room at a wayside inn. Sam and Paxton shared a chaff pallet on the floor. Sam wrapped his arms around his brother to help keep Paxton warm. The bedding smelt of smoke and sweat and animals. All night, the floors creaked, and a freezing wind blew through the walls like they were no more than sheets drying on a line.

By morning, Paxton's fever had returned. He rode atop the buckboard with Granny Peg and Isabella.

At Bristol, the caravan took the southeast fork toward Greenville, Tennessee. It was an uneven, rutted track that braved a dense forest. Sam took notice of changes in the other travelers. Sometimes, tall, erect, dark-skinned men passed with colorful scarves on their heads and bright sashes around their waists. They rode spirited ponies and traveled easily among the trappers with their packhorses or the traders with carts out, plying wares among the settlers and Indians alike.

Fallen trees had to be moved more often, along with deep holes and large rocks to be avoided, but during long stretches, Sam could still daydream or sing or recite his favorite poems. The weather held until they neared the crossing at Holston River. Then a storm blew in and assaulted the caravan with pea-sized hail. Ma told Sam to stop at the next tavern or inn.

The DeWoody Tavern had a room, but the rates were double what they'd paid in Virginia. When his mother objected to the price, a squat redheaded man huffed at her.

"You isn't in ol' Virginny anymore," he said.

Ma counted the coin from her purse.

The small man took the money. "Your Negro woman can stay in the barn."

"Oh no. I need her for my daughter," Ma said.

"Look here, I got no dog in the fight. I isn't a Quaker or a slaver, mind you, but I got to keep up my reputation as a clean establishment."

Ma ripped Isabella from Granny Peg's arms. Sam's sister began to whimper then cry loudly.

"My daughter needs her Granny Peg!" his mother shouted. "Otherwise, nobody will get any rest here."

Others in the tavern turned to stare. Sam swallowed hard.

The innkeeper's eyes narrowed. "How do I know you own her? You maybe stole her."

Ma reached inside her cape and pulled out a paper and handed it to the little man. "This is a copy of my father's will. It's certified by the clerk of Rockbridge County."

The innkeeper appeared to scrutinize the document, but the way his eyes flitted from top to bottom, Sam knew the man couldn't read.

"The Negro is a dollar extra."

His mother retrieved the paper before she handed over another coin. "I have taken note of your greed and craven ways," she said.

The man pocketed the coin. "Nobody gives a hoot what you

think."

Ma lifted her chin. "I am Elizabeth Blair Paxton Houston, sir."

"You kin to Sheriff Houston?"

"Yes, and this is not the last you will hear of my family."

A fearsome pride bloomed in Sam's chest. He had never loved and admired his mother more than at that moment.

The following day, large drifts of snow narrowed the road leading away from the tavern. The wagons advanced slowly under a silence broken only by the pleasant crunching from the horses' hooves breaking the crust of ice covering the path. Few travelers were about. Midday, they reached the Nolichucky River. Sam's teeth had been chattering for hours, and his knuckles were cracked and bloody. His heavy wool cape couldn't stop the sting from a relentless wind. Treacherous floes drifted in the river, and the ferry was closed. The only place to shelter was a cabin that served as a small general store and home to the ferryman and his wife.

The whole family had to sleep among barrels in the storeroom. The next morning, they woke to a soft snow that turned to rain as the day wore on. Sam sat on the floor by the one small hearth in the cabin. Paxton leaned against him while Sam read aloud by the light of a candle:

> "Achilles' wrath, to Greece the direful spring
> Of woes unnumber'd, heavenly goddess, sing!
> That wrath which hurl'd to Pluto's gloomy reign
> The souls of mighty chiefs untimely slain;
> Whose limbs unburied on the naked shore,
> Devouring dogs and hungry vultures tore."

John came to the hearth to warm himself. "Sam, where'd you get that candle?"

"Ma said I could use it."

"She shouldn't let you waste it on a silly book."

"Only you, in your ignorance, would declare that Achilles is silly."

John scoffed. "I'm your guardian, remember. Wait until we get to Tennessee. When we're on my land, I'm going to teach you to show some respect and keep your nose to the grindstone for once in your sorry life."

Sam snorted loudly. "Another declaration of ignorance. For your enlightenment, brother John, we have been in Tennessee the last three days."

"You know what I meant."

"It's not your land. It's all of ours," Paxton said.

With that, John left them alone.

The weather cleared the next day, and they crossed the Nolichucky River that afternoon. The following day, they took another ferry to cross the French Broad. Pushing onward under a brilliant blue sky, they were surrounded by soft brown hills except for patches of pine and spruce. Their last stop would be at Houston Station, about ten miles south of Maryville. It was named after one of the Major's uncles, another Matthew Houston, the one who had married a Lyle. His son, James, had taken over the place after his father's death.

Sam slowed the wagon at the turnoff near Nine Mile Creek. He pulled the leader left onto a hard-packed path. In a clearing ahead, he saw the palisade. The gates were opened, and Sam drove the wagon into a large courtyard. Cousin James came to greet the family. He was a man of middle age with the characteristic features of a Houston—sturdy frame, wavy chestnut hair, and a rosy bloom on his cheeks.

After a bountiful supper of fresh meat and winter vegetables straight from the ground, Sam and his brothers were given a room with a fireplace and two feather beds. At breakfast the next morning, Sam met three cousins, brothers all around his age. The hot food and warm bed and new friends changed Sam's outlook. He began to think happily of the new adventures he could have in Tennessee.

After a day of rest, the caravan left Houston Station to conquer the last few miles of their journey. They followed a less-traveled path leading west beyond the road they'd taken from Maryville.

Cousin James and Ma walked not far from Sam. A talkative man, Cousin James told the story of how Houston Station came to be.

"A Captain Martin ordered a fort built at my father's farm to protect against the aggression of the Cherokee. I was twenty-five. It was in the summer of eighty-eight when we were attacked and held under siege by those savages. John Sevier came to our rescue. God rest his soul." Turning to Ma, he said, "Since the garrison moved south to Hiwassee, we don't have trouble with the Cherokee anymore."

"How far away from the Indian territory are we?" Ma asked.

"A good ten miles south, across the Little Tennessee River. Don't fret about the Indians, Cousin Elizabeth. You have family all around your land. Joseph McConnel, he's a Quaker now, is on your southern border. You'll have no problem with him. He'll likely preach to you about having a slave. His mother was a Houston. The same for Samuel McKee, and the Edmondstons are kin to the Paxtons, I hear."

Again, Sam would be surrounded by relatives.

"You have good water, and it's well timbered, plenty of game. Last fall, I took the liberty of clearing a site for a cabin. There's a nice spring just below it. I haven't been up there in a while, but I recall there's a stand of red oak that will make a fine home for you."

They reached the stake that marked a corner of their four hundred nineteen acres. The path virtually disappeared in a tangle of bramble and briar.

Cousin James looked around. "I cut a way in somewhere around here."

John dismounted the sorrel mare and hacked at the thick vines with the sword he'd inherited from their father. He couldn't make a clean cut.

"You'll have to unload the wagons here," Cousin James said.

"Surely, we can manage the wagons that way." John pointed to the southwest.

"There's a canebrake down below," Cousin James said.

James came off the buckboard wagon. "The big mare could clear a path through it."

"That cane is ten feet tall and full of rattlesnakes. There's a path here somewhere. North is the direction we need to take."

While his brothers argued with Cousin James, Sam scoured the area around the wagons, finding evidence of a game trace or the path Cousin James had made. Either way, it led north. Sam released the dark bay from its harness and lifted Polly up to sit the horse. He gave her a fistful of the bay's mane. Then he hoisted Eliza up and placed her behind Polly. After that, Sam unhitched Goose and helped Paxton mount the big mare. Isabella giggled excitedly when Sam sat her in front of Paxton. Seeing his sister smiling and happy made Sam think his father might have been right to leave Isabella a horse in his will.

His brothers were still debating whether the wagons could make the trip through the canebrake.

"My dear guardians, you're wasting daylight. I've found a trace we can follow." Sam intentionally mimicked the way his mother would admonish his father.

John's face went red, and James shook his head.

Sam showed Cousin James the faint trail he'd found.

"Yes, this looks about right."

Sam took the bay horse by the bridle and started into the dense undergrowth. "Keep your head down," he told Polly and Eliza. Carefully, Sam pushed aside the limbs and brush that impeded the horse's way. Cousin James was not far behind, leading the mare with Paxton and Isabella.

It was slow going, and at one point, Sam thought he'd lost the trail and had to retrace his steps a few yards. The path veered slightly to the west, and suddenly, through the trees, an open area appeared. Cousin James had been true to his word. The clearing was bathed in sunlight and nicely situated on a hill. Sam helped Polly and Eliza dismount.

"It's good to have my feet on the ground again," Paxton said.

Cousin James pointed at a thicket of sweet gum trees. "A spring is hidden in there. It feeds a nice creek."

Ma and Granny Peg arrived next, each carrying some of the fresh provisions received at Houston Station.

"Thank you, Sam," Ma said. "I fear we would still be talking if you hadn't found the trail."

Sam and Paxton took the horses down to the creek for water. When they returned, William had brought up the cow.

When John reached the clearing, he rode close to Sam, saying, "Don't be getting full of yourself. It was luck, nothing more."

Sam shook his head and started for the wagons. He passed Robert and James, each leading a horse. Neither said a word to him. They spent hours traveling the quarter mile from the campsite to the wagons. Cousin James left in the midafternoon with a promise to bring his team the next day to widen the path for the wagons.

After the horses were fed and hobbled, Sam went to his mother. She had a small fire going while Granny Peg sliced bacon. Fresh eggs, milk, butter, and loaves of bread from Cousin James's store were laid out on a blanket. Isabella was sitting on the ground. Nearby, James and John were huddled over the survey papers Cousin James had given them.

"Where's Paxton?" Sam asked.

Ma pointed east. "He took the girls to gather more wood."

Sam scanned the area as he walked. Robert and William were up the hill with the horses. In the northern sky, a flock of starlings flew together like a black ribbon, weaving and folding and changing shapes that darkened and then dispersed just as quickly.

As Sam entered the woods, Polly ran up to him. "Paxton's hurting," she cried. "I didn't know what to do."

Sam sprinted ahead and found Paxton hunched over at the waist. His hands were on his knees as he gasped for air. Eliza stood frozen with a bundle of sticks and branches in her arms. Sam bent down over Paxton. His brother's lips were blue, his face ashen. Sam knelt low on the ground so that Paxton could lean onto his back. Then Sam rose to his feet and looped his arms under Paxton's knees. Paxton's labored breathing filled Sam's ears.

"Polly, you and Eliza run ahead. Tell Ma."

Polly picked up the small load of wood she'd collected, and she and Eliza started toward the campsite. Sam walked as quickly as he could. He desperately wanted his brother to regain his strength, hoping Paxton's health might be restored with enough rest and tranquility. It had to, for Sam hated to see his brother suffer.

Ma hurried to meet Sam and led him to a place where she had spread out another blanket. Sam gently laid Paxton on the ground. His color had restored some. As his mother tended to Paxton, Sam felt helpless watching his brother struggle for breath. It was too painful to bear, and he retreated.

Sam climbed up the hill, passing the horses and his brothers. When he reached the top, he stood on the edge of the tree line. Swaths of gray-blue clouds floated over the mountains in the east. The sun's last rays struck the lower hills, casting the contours of the land in high relief. He marveled at what lay hidden in those mountains. The thought of exploring their new home eased his mind. Cousin James had said the Cherokee boundary was only ten miles away. Sam could find adventures close to home while Paxton had time to heal. Then they would leave for the west or wherever offered the best prospect of fortune and fame.

A terrible shriek broke the silence.

Sam ran down the hill in a panic, afraid of what had happened. The screaming grew louder and more wretched. He saw Granny Peg's dark silhouette out near the grazing horses.

Ma ran toward Granny Peg. By the time Sam joined her, Robert and William were there too.

Isabella lay motionless on the ground.

As James and John arrived, Granny Peg cried out, "Oh, Miss Elizabeth, our girl is hurt. I was taking her to the creek, and she went too close to Goose."

Ma knelt down and gently turned Isabella's head. The other side of Isabella's face was a bloody mess. A hoof had broken the bone clean through where her left eye should have been. Ma gasped loudly and sat back on her heels then burst forth with a scream that shook Sam to his core. Lost in grief, his mother rocked back and forth, sobbing.

Polly and Eliza ran toward them. Sam called out, "Go back to Paxton."

They didn't leave, however, but stayed standing timidly at a distance.

Granny Peg dropped to her knees next to Ma and took hold of her arm. "I didn't mean to get her killed."

"Oh, Peggy. It's not your fault," Ma cried. "It's mine."

They all stood by silently as tears wet Ma's face. She looked up at the sky as though talking to God. "I prayed so hard to bear a daughter, and he punished me for my vanity. My sweet Isabella had to pay for my sins. Now, the angels have taken her from me. Blessed be her soul."

All through the journey and his father's death, Ma had been strong and stoic, never once complaining. Hearing her talk of the guilt she'd carried for Isabella's deformity unsettled him, as though some curtain had been pulled back, allowing Sam to see the heavy burden his mother had borne for years.

"Oh, Miss Elizabeth. Please don't sell me now," Granny Peg

pleaded.

Ma turned to her, a fragile smile on her lips. "Why would I sell you?"

"Cause if Isabella is gone, you aren't goin' to need me so much anymore."

His mother took Granny Peg's hands in hers. "I've known you since the day you were born. No one else understands me like you do. Besides, who is going to care for me when all these children get married and leave?"

That set Granny Peg to wailing. "Oh no! Miss Elizabeth, who's goin' to care for me? All my children have been left in Virginia."

Eliza ran to Granny Peg and grabbed her skirt. "Don't cry, Granny Peg. I'll take care of you. I promise."

Sam watched as his mother carefully turned Isabella's head to hide the crushed side. She then straightened Isabella's dress. He had to look away. His mother's long-submerged emotions were disturbing and frightening and too deep to fathom all at once. Hearing about the fears Ma had never talked about made Sam worry that other dark secrets were swimming beneath the surface.

A nearly full moon rose over the eastern ridge, above the clouds that hugged the peaks. The moonlight illuminated the ground well past midnight as Sam and his brothers prepared Isabella's grave. After the moon traveled into the western sky, the family bedded down under blankets spread around the fire. Sam lay between Paxton and Polly. His arms cradled his head as it struck him that the first spade of earth he'd turned in Tennessee wasn't to prepare a field or plant a seed. It had been for his sister's grave. He felt sad about Isabella dying, but the feeling was colored by the shock of hearing Ma confess the heavy guilt she'd kept to herself.

If God had punished his mother for wanting a daughter, had caused her to suffer mightily for her supposed sin, he didn't know how anyone could ever find a reprieve from the harshness of life. Then something came to him—as he'd been running toward Granny Peg, Sam had immediately assumed Paxton was the one who'd been hurt or died. His pulse quickened as he relived that moment of terror. But his fear subsided with the reassuring sound of his brother's steady breathing. He fell asleep with the pleasant thought of roaming their new land and exploring every creek and hollow hidden in the magical hills around him.

Chapter Five

One fine spring morning, the plow stood idle, and a team of horses grazed while Sam sat under a hickory tree, reading. Above him, perched on a limb, a mockingbird sang its long, complicated song as the clear, bright light illuminated the pages of the book resting in Sam's lap. On his first reading of *The Iliad*, Sam had raced through the poem with a fever. Now, he wanted to savor each word, letting the syllables roll off his tongue as he read his favorite passages out loud.

The epic drama had captured his imagination and taken him to a faraway place with its many heroes and battles. While reading, Sam's spirit soared, his heart open to all the possibilities in the fantastical world of Homer. Perhaps someday, he could read *The Iliad* in Greek or Latin and so hear the story as it was originally told. He had begun to notice a bountiful use of the word *main* in Pope's translation, and he yearned to know the words straight from Homer's pen.

But he couldn't tell anyone of his ambitions. Not his guardian brothers—they would heap scorn and abuse on him if he announced he wanted to study the classical languages. He couldn't tell Paxton, either. That would be an admission neither wanted to make. Their dream of venturing off together had died some time before, but Sam pretended his brother would recover, and Paxton went along with the lie. His mother wouldn't understand his desire to become a scholar. Sam didn't know whom to turn to for guidance about his future.

"Sam!" His mother's voice carried from a distance.

Ma came marching across the half-plowed field, her skirt and apron gathered in her hands and lifted to avoid the cockleburs. Like sentries, John and James walked on either side of her. This unannounced visit had all the markings of what his mother had begun to call the "family council." Whatever came out of these councils was never to Sam's advantage. So he didn't budge but just turned the page.

"I told you, Ma," John said.

"Why aren't you working?" Ma dropped her skirts and wiped her forehead with her sleeve.

Sam got to his feet. "I was taking a short rest."

As John grunted, James said, "That's all you ever do—sleep, eat, and read."

"I've done my share." Sam put the book in his knapsack.

"Hush." Ma looked at Sam directly. "Your brothers and I…"

That detestable phrase was the prelude to each attempt by his brothers to force Sam to do their bidding.

"Have decided you can give up the farm work for now."

That was better news than he'd expected.

"But you're to apprentice in a trade store," James said.

What was left of their father's estate had been invested in a small trading house and general store in Maryville. Nothing fancy or interesting was there, just sacks of flour, sugar, coffee, and cornmeal.

"How am I going to be educated if I have to work all the time?"

James scoffed. "We're not paying for any more of your education."

"Reverend Moore says you didn't do your lessons," Ma said.

At Porter Academy, the lessons, especially the arithmetic, were tedious and uninteresting. More often than not, exploring the woods had taken precedence over the schoolhouse.

"It's not our fault you wasted your time," John added.

"You're going to work for Mr. Sheffy at Southwest Point. He has agreed to let you apprentice with him." His mother clasped her hands together. "I've made arrangements for you to leave today. You'll board with your father's cousin, Mr. McEwen."

John moved in closer and poked a finger into Sam's chest. He now had to look up to Sam, but that didn't stop him from acting the big man. "There will be no more slouching on the job, hear me? Mr. Sheffy will have his eye on you, so mind yourself."

"Don't embarrass the family," Ma said.

Sam fumed inside, but he'd been cornered and couldn't openly defy his mother. Since their arrival in Tennessee, she no longer made exceptions for him, not with Paxton nearly bedridden and Robert's frequent trips back to Virginia. Expected to be a workhorse, Sam had the nature of a wild stallion, footloose and fancy-free.

"Peggy has dinner for you. Mr. Norwood will take you to Southwest Point," Ma said.

Sam went to Paxton, where he rested on a daybed in the shade of the cabin breezeway.

"I'm being sent away," Sam said.

Paxton raised up on one elbow and held out his other hand. Sam grabbed it but couldn't bring himself to say anything, so he sat down on the edge of the bed, still holding Paxton's hand.

"If you don't come back, I'll understand. This could be your chance to go west, find your fame and fortune."

"Not without you. Cause I don't need the fortune. I'd just give it all to Ma anyway."

"Sam!" Granny Peg came hustling up the steps. "There you is. I'm supposed to give you your dinner. Now, come on to the kitchen."

Sam rose and gave Paxton's hand a squeeze before letting go. "I'll be back. I promise."

Sam collected his food in the kitchen, half a loaf of bread and a thick slice of ham.

Granny Peg huffed and said, "It's goin' to be awful quiet around here. Nobody else likes to stir the pot like you, Sam."

Wearing a straw hat on his head, Sam set out with his knapsack and all his worldly possessions—a flintlock rifle, a knife, his book, and a spare calico shirt. The path went by a meadow filled with wild strawberries growing in patches like islands in the short grass. He stopped every few yards, and soon, his hands were stained a deep red. A little farther on, he came upon a flock of geese feeding in a field of budding corn. Sam took off running at them for the fun of it and to save a neighbor's crop. If he'd discovered one blessing in moving to Tennessee, it was that he had found a small cadre of second and third cousins near his age. In the first month of their arrival, family and neighbors, one and the same, helped to build their dogtrot cabin. Once the trees were felled and the stumps and roots dug out, the land gave up bounties of corn, wheat, barley, and a kitchen garden that kept the family well fed. By late autumn, they had a barn, chicken coop, paddock, pens, smokehouse, kitchen, and loom room, all in good working order.

After the harvest came in, the small troupe of Houston cousins, with Sam as leader of the pack, were free for a time. During late fall and all winter, the cousins combed the woods for miles, from Sam's house down to Houston Station, crisscrossing hundreds of acres, finding arrowheads, old baskets, and animal bones, evidence of the Cherokees who had lived on and hunted that very same ground.

Sam was annoyed that the boundary with the Cherokee territory lay close by, just across the Little Tennessee River, a mere spitting distance from their farm, yet he was forbidden to go south because his mother feared he would be kidnapped. He wanted to wander the hills again and see the understory woodland where spring flowers bloomed—the light pink of mountain laurel, the brilliant flame of azalea, the broad flush of colorful rhododendrons, and the pure white of star magnolia—in colors that burst through the fresh bright green of the new leaves on the trees. A sort of reverie would come to him when he felt free of the trappings of civilization, like chores, classes, and the need for coin. But now, instead of exploring the fringes of Cherokee territory, he would be a prisoner to this Mr. Sheffy in Southwest Point.

As he approached the turnoff to the store where Mr. Norwood waited, Sam walked farther north, in the direction of Porter Academy. No harm would come of having one last hour of freedom before his sentence as a store clerk began. The schoolhouse door was open. Two students, an older man and the young son of the town blacksmith, were inside with the schoolmaster. Sam stood in the doorway and waited for Reverend Moore to pause the lesson. He then approached the old schoolmaster and quickly stated his desire to learn Greek.

"So I can read Homer in his native language," he explained.

"I didn't take you for a scholar. You've a sound mind for reading, no doubt. Why now? You didn't do your lessons before."

Sam was tired of hearing people say he'd wasted his time. He refused to accept that being in nature and exploring the world was wasteful.

Reverend Moore placed a hand on Sam's shoulder and walked Sam back toward the door. "You must learn geometry and the sciences before you can tackle the ancient languages."

"I can do my sums easy enough. Why do I need to know how to measure the distance to the moon?"

"That's not all geometry is good for. Before you can advance, you will need to become as familiar with Euclid as you are with Homer. Are you prepared to do that?"

Sam moped away, his footsteps heavy with frustration. His brothers, James and John, would surely hear of his request to study Greek. Without a doubt, the Holy Apostles would mock Sam when they heard about his request. *But what does that matter now?* All he could think about was how to avoid spending the next five years at the beck and call of every knucklehead who wanted a pound of cornmeal or a yard of calico.

Mr. Sheffy turned out to be an enormous man with pitch-black hair, a large bulbous nose, and a loud and ready laugh. For three months, Sam labored under his tutelage, learning to measure and weigh with accuracy, witness notes and debts, calculate interest, and keep the account book—the primary tasks needed to run a successful trade and mercantile store.

People came in from all over the surrounding territory—Cherokee, Creek, Chickasaw, and Muskogee. Sam quickly picked up the universal sign language of pointing, nodding, and using his hands for sizing and fingers for numbers. And one phrase—*hee la gu*—seemed very common, meaning "how much" or "how many."

Once Sheffy deemed his apprentice sufficiently trained, he sent Sam home with the parting words, "Come back if you like. I can always put you to work."

At the height of summer, Sam returned to the Baker Creek farm with experience and another book, *Gulliver's Travels*. He immediately asked about Paxton and found his brother dozing in a chair by the hearth in the kitchen.

Before he could even get through the door, Granny Peg put a finger to her lips and in a half whisper scolded Sam, "Don't come in here and wake my boy."

A terrible foreboding caused a sudden chill—the way she said "my boy" was the same way Granny Peg had talked about Isabella, as though Paxton were a cripple who needed her full attention.

Paxton stirred. "Sam, you're back?"

"I'd never leave without you, brother."

Paxton grabbed Sam's forearm. "I wouldn't have been angry if you had."

His brother was admitting he would never be able to seek his fortune in the West, and it stabbed at Sam's heart. He tried to say something encouraging, to tell Paxton he would be right as rain in no time, but the words stuck in his throat.

"Don't wait for me, Sam. Someday soon, you'll have to strike off on your own."

The next day, Sam went to work in the store with Mr. Norwood. Maryville seemed a world away from Sheffy's. Dull and monotonous, the only trade came from local families and the occasional rover who traveled in from the Carolinas. Bored most days, Sam missed the activity at Sheffy's. Worse, Mr. Norwood was a dour man with no sense of humor. He treated Sam as though he were still an apprentice, expecting him to do all the heavy lifting, restocking shelves, moving barrels, and sweeping up the floor, but he wouldn't let him near the account book.

One afternoon, after Sam unpacked crates from a potter in Greenville, his brother John showed up to manage the store because Mr. Norwood had business in Knoxville.

"I don't need watching over," Sam groused.

"Mind your mouth," John said as a customer came in.

Sam recognized the man from Sheffy's. They exchanged nods of familiarity. Sam knew him as John Rogers, the half-breed son of a white man who'd gone to live among the Cherokee after fighting in the Revolutionary War. That day, Rogers was wearing a colorful sash around his waist, and his thick black hair fell to his shoulders. The long rifle he carried had elaborate silver markings on the stock. Two young boys came in with him. They had the same black hair with darker complexions. Rogers turned and said a few sharp Cherokee words that sent the boys scurrying back to the open door. Sam made a pretense of sweeping the floor and moved closer to where Rogers stood at the counter.

Rogers told John, "I have skins to trade for iron bars."

His brother didn't look up. "I only take coin for iron."

"I have coin."

John kept his eyes on the account book. "Don't have any iron to sell today."

Sam turned his attention to the boys waiting quietly in the doorway. He pantomimed shooting birds out of the sky with the broomstick. The smaller boy broke his solemn posture, and the older one smiled. They both took a few tentative steps inside.

John's voice rose loudly. "No, we don't have saltpeter, either."

Sam glanced over at John. "We have some in the storeroom."

A deep scowl on his face, his brother said, "He's mistaken. We don't have any powder."

"Yes, we do!" Sam started for the door, telling Rogers, "Let's see what you have." They went to a packhorse tethered by the water trough.

His brother stood in the doorway.

Rogers had several bundles of hides—deer, beaver, and black bear. Sam judged them to be worth a dollar or more and knew a good trade could be had at the right measure of saltpeter.

"I need needles and salt too," Rogers said.

Sam nodded. "I'll give you a fair trade."

He left Rogers outside to deal with untying the bundles from the packhorse.

Once inside the store, John came close to Sam, hissing in his ear, "We do not sell iron or saltpeter to murdering savages!"

"Sheffy trades with him."

John couldn't keep from sputtering when he cried out, "You're in my store now. Best you remember my rules."

"I have a share too."

"Don't forget that I have twice as much as you."

John stayed behind the counter while Sam weighed the saltpeter on the scale. After Rogers left with the supplies, John wouldn't let Sam enter the trade in the account book. He had to watch while his brother valued the bundles at half a dollar.

"Those skins are worth more."

"He's an Indian. He's bound to have cheated you."

Furious, Sam went outside and sat on the stoop. In the sunlight, he inspected the deer hides. They'd been brain-tanned and were of good quality. The bearskin was small. He held up two beaver skins and went to stand in the doorway.

"A hatter will pay half a dollar just for the beavers. With the deer and bear, that bundle is worth over a dollar!"

John came and took the beaver skins from Sam just as an unfamiliar wagon pulled to a stop at the water trough. The two mares looked in need of tending. They were thick with sweat around the collars and had bony hips and sagging spines.

The driver, a man of large girth, stepped down, letting out a grunt.

"I'll need feed, boy," he told Sam. As the man walked toward the store, he yelled, "Ned! Get the bucket." An older black man rose from the wagon bed.

Sam stepped aside as the large man swaggered through the door. His broadcloth coat had shiny spots at the elbows and a tattered hem.

John greeted the driver like royalty. "What can I do for you today, sir?"

A pungent, earthy smell billowed out from the old man as he handed off the feed bucket. Sam went inside to fill the bucket with a mixture of barley, corn, and oats from a barrel.

The trader asked John, "You got any iron to trade?"

"I'll need coin for it," John replied.

Sam blurted, "You said we didn't have any iron!"

The large man turned to Sam. "Who's running this store?"

John blustered, "He's a clerk. I'm the owner. We have iron."

"I don't have the coin, but I know a blacksmith willing to pay dearly. We can share the profits."

John squinted.

The trader lowered his chin with a knowing look. "Ever since the authorities closed down Earle's mine in Chattooga, the Cherokee are eager to trade for it."

John reared his head back. "We don't sell iron to Indians. Not so they can make rifles to kill our people."

The trader inspected his fingers. "I never said the blacksmith was an Indian." He looked up at John, smiling. "I am simply explaining the conditions of *le marché*. And if my name's not French Moran, I don't know who else can be trusted to give an honest opinion about what people are wanting these days. There's not a single trader from here to Charlestown, white or red, who's more willing to share the intelligence garnered from his travels."

John pursed his lips tight.

"It's the wise trader who knows when *la pomme est mûre.*" Moran turned to Sam and said through the corner of his mouth, "That's when the apple is ripe for picking."

"Well, I guess I could let you have one bar. But I'll need some surety."

Moran puffed up his chest. "My name is my surety. My word is my bond."

John walked out from behind the counter. Sam followed the two men outside, carrying the bucket of feed. He handed the bucket to Ned, and the old man moved toward the weary nags.

John went to inspect the bundle of skins.

Moran leaned on the wagon. "You hear they killed James Vann?"

"Who's he?" Sam asked.

"The richest man in Cherokee Territory. A mixed breed out of Georgia."

John lifted the first hide. "Those people are no better than the full-blooded savages."

"Vann conducted his life in the same style as many a Southern white planter. Could have taught a thing or two to the settlers around here." Moran winked at Sam.

John announced, "I can let you have one bar on credit." He then turned to Sam. "Go fetch the iron."

"You said we don't have iron, so go get it yourself."

"You couldn't find it anyway." John huffed off.

"Why did they kill him?" Sam asked.

"When he drank, Vann was a mean, vengeful man. Even his mother was afraid of what he would do. They say it's family who killed him." Moran reached under the wagon seat to remove a large leather flagon, pulled out the stopper, and took a long draw.

"They killed Vann like they killed Doublehead although for different reasons."

"Doublehead?" Sam had heard that name before from Cousin James.

"After a ball play at the Hiwassee Garrison, Bone Cracker accused

Doublehead of taking a bribe from Colonel Meigs. Bone went at Doublehead with a hatchet, but Doublehead shot Bone with a pistol. Some say Hell Fire Jack was in on it, but the Ridge is who finally killed that mean old snake, Doublehead."

"Was Doublehead the one who attacked Cavitt's Station?" Sam remembered the story about a massacre years earlier.

"Ah yes, that was an ugly affair. His own people named him 'baby killer' after that. He already had a bad reputation after he and his brother, Pumpkin Boy, scalped those men in Kentucky. They skinned them alive, like they were game, then roasted and ate their flesh."

The revolting thought raised gooseflesh on Sam's arms, but a certain fascination took over when he remembered cannibals did live on distant islands. Never once had he considered it here.

"The natives believe if you eat your enemy, you become strong like them," Moran added, as though he'd read Sam's thoughts.

John returned with the one iron bar in hand.

Moran offered the flagon to John, who shook his head.

"No?" the old trader said with a shrug. "It's good rum. Quite sublime." He then offered the flagon to Sam.

Before Sam could even consider taking a sip, John motioned toward the skins. "Put these in the storeroom."

Reluctantly, Sam took the bundle. He could see the skins weren't worth near the value of the iron bar, poorly tanned and only four of them. He didn't move to take them inside, not wanting to miss anything else Moran had to say about the Cherokee.

The wagon creaked when Moran stepped up to the seat.

John went into the store, but Sam stayed near the wagon.

Moran looked down at Sam. "*La vie est trop courte pour voire du mauvais vin.*"

"What's that mean?"

"Life's too short to drink bad wine. Or in my case, rum." Moran took up the reins. "Don't get stuck here, son, else you'll fall prey to the *ennui* and waste your life."

Slowly, the wagon rolled away. The sun had fallen below the tree line, and within a few moments, all evidence of French Moran had vanished in the gloom.

Sam took the bundle of skins inside, scoffing loudly. "These aren't worth a copper."

John closed the account book. "I'll be the judge of that." His brother picked up the beaver skins, saying, "Sweep up that feed you dropped." He moved to the door. "My key is under the counter. I hope I can trust you to lock up before you leave."

"Where are you taking the beavers?"

"To the hatter—see what I can get for them."

Sam shook his head in disgust. Alone then, he swept with a fury, pounding the bristles against the plank floor. He hated to think that he would be stuck there for another five years. No matter how much he knew about trading, Sam would be relegated to the menial tasks, held back and shut down every time he tried to assert himself. Having to heed his brother's opinion about who was good and who wasn't made it all the worse. He didn't see why he should feel animosity toward Rogers and the young boys with him. After hearing French Moran, Sam only wanted to know more about the Cherokees. Those strange, exotic names—Doublehead, Pumpkin Boy, Bone Cracker, the Ridge, Hell Jack Fire—were as tantalizing as the heroes in *The Iliad*.

He recalled one line when Achilles declared to Agamemnon:
"What cause have I to war at thy decree?
The distant Trojans never injured me..."

Sam felt the same. He should have the freedom to decide for himself who was friend and who was foe. He threw the broom to the floor and kicked the nearest barrel. He refused to waste his life in a dark storeroom where everything was the same and all he ever saw were sacks of flour, bolts of calico, and people who looked just like him. He was sixteen. James was twenty-five, and John was twenty-three, but his brothers wouldn't be leaving Baker Creek anytime soon.

Sam quickly gathered some provisions: a blanket, dried beef and venison, shot and gunpowder, hooks and twine, a small round mirror, and a flint to sharpen his knife. He listed it all in the account book. In an unexpected moment of pride, Sam wrote his name with a flourish in the column for Debtor as though he'd crossed a threshold into manhood.

At the last minute, he added to his debt three packets of needles.

He bolted outside, afraid he might lose his nerve. He closed the door hastily, turned the lock, and slid John's key through the gap under the door. The thought of John being locked out of the store brought a chuckle. John would probably have to wait for Mr. Norton to open the store the next day. With his prized books in his knapsack, his rifle and knife, and a few days' provisions, he took the road in the same direction French Moran's wagon had gone.

A cool breeze brushed his cheeks, and a pair of doves flew overhead as though late for Sunday meeting. The trilling of crickets filled the air. Bats swooped and dipped in the coming night sky, and lightning bugs flickered among the trees, like sprites welcoming Sam to his freedom.

Sam followed the main road south to the Little Tennessee. A large waning half-moon hovered low in the sky. A loud rushing sound came several moments before he saw the river. He removed his boots and let his bare feet feel their way over the rocky shoal.

Moonlight rippled on the waves of water, and in the distance, the soothing call of a whippoorwill sounded. A sense of the wider world took hold, and Sam stopped and lifted his face toward a thousand stars in the night sky. The restless torrent pushed against his calves, and he felt strong, invincible, and immortal. A powerful premonition possessed his whole being—the future ahead would turn out for the best because things do happen for a reason. Sam spread his arms wide as though he could embrace all the knowledge available to men. Beauty and simplicity laced with hardship and contradictions—that was the nature of life as Sam felt it.

When he reached the other side, he settled onto the ground under the shelter of a tree with a limb hanging out over a pool of calm water. Sleep wouldn't come, and he heard a strange noise. His heartbeat quickened as he considered what danger might be nearby. He turned his head in the opposite direction and heard it again, very near. Scared out of his wits, he sat still and alert, listening closely. He moved ever so slightly, heard the sound once more, then realized it was his hat brushing against the blanket he wore around his shoulders.

His body relaxed, but he didn't fall into a light sleep until well after the moon dipped low in the sky. A loud splash woke him just before dawn. In the gray light, a figure appeared upstream. Sam recognized Rogers, who was hauling a cone-shaped basket from the river. Quickly, he flipped the trap upside down, and fish tumbled out onto the ground. His two young boys were with him and hurried to grab a hold of them, giggling and squealing.

Seeing Sam, Rogers motioned for him to follow to where they were camped only a few yards away. French Moran was there, sitting on the back of his wagon while Ned tended the fire.

"Well, this is a surprise." Moran was holding his flagon in his hand.

Sam nodded, saying, "How do you do, Mr. Moran?"

Why are they together? Are they in cahoots, out to rob or swindle someone? Moran, he could see, might have been cooking something up, but John Rogers he knew as an honest tradesman. As the outsider, the stranger to this world, Sam kept his suspicions, vague as they were, to himself.

"Did your man send you after the iron?" Moran asked. "Once he'd realized we'd never come to terms to share the profit?"

"He's my brother. And, no, I'm out exploring."

"Your brother's a fool and a bigot," Moran said to Sam.

"You told the truth," Rogers said as he worked at preparing the two stripers and a large catfish. He shoved sticks stripped of bark into their mouths and laid them directly on the coals.

"What's your name?" Moran asked.

"Samuel Houston, sir. But I go by Sam 'cause my father was Samuel."

Rogers mixed cornmeal and water into a thick mush. He pressed it onto more of the branches stripped of bark, giving one stick to each boy to hold over the coals.

The roasting fish smelled divine. After a few minutes, Rogers pulled the stripers off the coals and laid them on a large flat rock, where they steamed in the cool morning air. He carefully turned the catfish over and gave it another minute on the coals.

Once all the food was ready, they gathered around and shared the meal freely.

Moran licked his fingers. "A good trader doesn't care a whit who he trades with, just as long as he can make a dollar out of you. There's no better man than John Rogers, here." He pointed at Rogers. "Not like his father Hell Jack Fire, who has a penchant for his rum. What about you?" He offered the flagon to Sam.

Upon hearing that Rogers didn't drink, Sam felt compelled to again forego a taste.

The old trader took another swig.

"The Cherokee could teach white folks a thing or two, especially the half-breeds, like my friend here. They got the right idea: pick the best from the civilized world and enjoy all the freedoms of the red man."

Moran continued wistfully, "But that life is on its way out. Pretty soon, all the Indians, not just the Cherokee, will be living like the white man. The Creeks, the Chickasaw, the Iroquois, and the Shawnee—the Indian way of life will be gone before we know it. A pity." He sighed.

"The Americans, so jealous of their own freedom, are blind to the plight of the red and black man alike. *C'est la vie.* All men are hypocrites to some degree."

Women too, Sam thought. If he'd known Moran better, Sam might have told the story of the old woman at Seven Mile Ford and how she treated her daughters like slaves, all the while preaching about freedom for Granny Peg.

They sat silent. Sam waited for the next move, unsure what to do.

"I've a wagon full of ginseng to trade for a cask of rum waiting in Charlestown. That's what the merchants want now, to sell to the Chinaman." Moran got to his feet, wobbling before gaining his balance. "Sam, since you're out exploring anyway, it would be a grand favor to me if you would accompany John Rogers to his destination. He's got three bars of iron and a good measure of saltpeter. Another man with a rifle will deter thieves and bandits."

Sam glanced at Rogers, who nodded in agreement. "I can do that favor." He didn't question where they were headed. He wanted a reason to stick with Rogers and the two boys.

French Moran let out a satisfied sigh then retired to the back of his wagon, lying down on the piles of ginseng. Ned climbed up and took the reins, and they were off toward the main road.

Sam had missed his chance to have a taste of rum, but he wouldn't tie his fortune to the old trader just for a sip of spirits, not after seeing how Moran cared for his horses. Not sure what to do next, feeling shy or something, he asked, "How do you know Mr. Moran?"

"My father knew him in the war. Moran was with the Americans, and my father fought with the British."

Rogers pushed dirt onto the fire. Then he worked quietly, wrapping the iron bars in a blanket and strapping them onto the packhorse. They took up a narrow trail heading southwest with Rogers in the lead and Sam in the rear, behind the two boys. Although he still hadn't asked where they were going, Sam was content as they traveled along a faint game trace. In the deep silence of the virgin woodland, where summer's heat couldn't penetrate, Sam had found his paradise. It was exactly what he'd dreamt about when the family first arrived in Tennessee.

Late that afternoon, Rogers led them to a small cave in a craggy hillside. He reached in and pulled out a hide-bound packet containing several yams. Rogers started a fire with a small stone and a bow. As the yams cooked in the coals, Sam shared the dried venison he carried in his knapsack. It was a light meal by his family's standards, yet Sam found he wasn't hungry.

Night came on, and they sat around the fire while Rogers spoke in Cherokee to his sons. Sam listened, not comprehending but finding the soft cadence of the language, full of oo's and ahh's and laa's, intriguing. He couldn't believe his good fortune. In a few days' time, he'd shot years ahead of his brothers. The pain of leaving Paxton came to him, but he buried it quickly.

The next morning, the trail descended into a valley, and after a full day, pausing only for water, they arrived at the mouth of a river that poured into the much bigger Tennessee. The smaller river flowed from the east, and the eons of silt and rocks carried down from the mountains had formed a large island. A swiftly moving channel separated the island from where Sam and Rogers stood.

Rogers placed his older son on the packhorse, and Sam hoisted the younger boy onto his shoulders. Together, they waded waist-deep into the water. A smattering of small huts clung to the tree line just beyond the shore. Rogers walked farther inland until they reached a cluster of log structures and more of the thatched huts. Rogers stopped in front of the largest cabin, a two-story dwelling.

In the gloaming, a tall man appeared. He wore an indigo-blue sash wrapped around his head, buckskin leggings, and a blanket draped over one shoulder. The man greeted Rogers. He then approached Sam and clasped Sam's arm with a strong, friendly hand, saying something in Cherokee.

Rogers translated. "He says you are Kalunah, the raven Oolooteka dreamt of last night."

Oolooteka said something else, and the men laughed.

"If you'd been an eagle, he'd have had to kill you."

Rogers and Oolooteka were both smiling. That put Sam at ease, although it was the strangest greeting he'd ever received. Truly, he was entering a peculiar and exciting new world.

"The white men call him Chief John Jolly, but the Cherokee know him as Oolooteka. It means 'he who put away the drum.'"

Oolooteka led them to an open area where a few men were building a fire. All seemed happy to see John Rogers, who then introduced Sam to the men as "Kalunah."

Oolooteka took his seat at the fire pit, and John Rogers sat next to him. Rogers motioned for Sam to sit too. A calico cat climbed into Oolooteka's lap, and he stroked it. A pipe passed among the men in silence. Then Oolooteka said something, and Rogers turned to Sam.

"Oolooteka invites you to speak to the village."

"What do I say?"

"Tell them your story."

Sam started to speak, but Rogers said, "It is customary to stand."

Sam rose to his feet, wiping his hands against his pants leg.

"I was born in Virginia. My father was a major in the militia before he died, and then we moved to Tennessee."

Rogers translated to Oolooteka and the others. A long silence ensued. Sam didn't know what to make of the lack of a reaction. Everyone was sitting comfortably, with no murmuring among the men. Then Oolooteka stood to speak, tears welling in his eyes.

Sam waited for Rogers to translate.

"Oolooteka is sorry for your father's death. His brother, The Bench, the redheaded brave warrior he dearly loved, died in Virginia."

The chief had a brother with red hair too! The coincidence stunned Sam.

He stood again, facing the chief directly. "I am sorry for your brother's death." Sam's voice cracked as water came to his own eyes.

Knowing he'd left Paxton behind brought a deep sorrow he couldn't ignore. This was the price of his adventure—the loss of an earlier dream.

The next day, Rogers prepared to leave Hiwassee Island. He gave Oolooteka two of the iron bars.

"I am going upriver to visit my father," Rogers told Sam. "Oolooteka invites you to stay here as his guest."

Sam had grown attached to Rogers and his young sons. For the first time since he ran away, Sam felt vulnerable. Then Oolooteka handed Sam a small drinking gourd, hollowed out with a knob on the stem that would serve as a handle.

"Oolooteka offers this gift as a sign of friendship," Rogers told Sam.

In return, Sam gave a packet of needles to Oolooteka. The chief's offer of a place to stay proved too good to turn down, and Sam didn't wish to appear ungrateful. Also, he didn't want to cling to Rogers out of cowardice.

Sam tried to sound casual when he asked, "Who else can translate on the island?"

"Little Otter will help you," Rogers answered.

After a few nights of sleeping on the floor in Oolooteka's cabin, Sam found a large elm tree on the western edge of the island. Near the sounds of the river and night birds, he slept easily instead of being surrounded by the snoring and rustling of others. Out there, he awoke to the delightful chatter of the young girls collecting water for the morning meal. From this vantage, Sam could also watch the comings and goings of the militia housed in a garrison across the Tennessee River.

One day, Little Otter, who did speak passable English, helped Sam construct a bark lean-to near an old woman's hut. While they were working, Sam learned her name had been *Awi Taleetama*, Little Wren. After she lost her husband and children from the smallpox, she howled in grief for months. They called her Howling Nancy after that.

Sam liked to watch her comb the watery terrace of land beyond the canebrakes, digging in the soft tidal banks for freshwater mussels and clams. She would collect them in a basket and then sit by her small wattle-and-daub hut, cracking the shells, eating the little morsels, then throwing the shells to one side. The mound of shells measured about half the size of her hut.

Cherokee women spent their time preparing food, tending their gardens, and doing handiwork: weaving baskets, sewing beads to adorn their clothing, and tanning hides. What surprised Sam the most was that Oolooteka owned a family of Negroes. They worked the fields and cared for the livestock. Even here, Jerry would not have been free to do as he pleased. He might have been a half-breed, just like Oolooteka, but Jerry was trapped by the color of his skin.

In a short time, Sam embraced the habits of Little Otter: rise at dawn, eat when hungry, and spend the day roaming the hills across the river, following the streams into valley crevices, mounting summits, and sometimes pretending to stalk an enemy, but always in pursuit of game. Even though Oolooteka's village had an abundance of cattle and hogs, the thrill of the chase called to the young men.

Most nights, a council fire was lit. The men, and sometimes a woman, would come to Oolooteka for assistance with a lost cow or a stolen gun or something. Around the fire, Sam absorbed the sounds when the Cherokee spoke. He began to pair the words with their meanings, recognizing the rhythms and inflections of the Cherokee language. After a few weeks of living on the island, Sam realized he could follow a story of the wampum and the Cherokee peace with the Iroquois.

Oolooteka kept a trade store where the villagers could exchange skins, crops, or baskets for articles of convenience brought from the white world—pocket mirrors, needles, thread, beads and ribbons, salt, sugar, and flour. On the shelves, Sam found a few books.

"Kalunah would like to borrow this." Sam held up *The Lay of the Last Minstrel*, by Walter Scott.

"Oolooteka doesn't read or write," the chief told him.

"How did you come by the books?"

"A white teacher brought them. He left the books but never built the schoolhouse."

Just then, a villager came and announced that a boat was coming across the river from the garrison. Oolooteka and Sam walked to the northern shore. They watched a scow cut through the current. Little Otter and some others joined them.

A man in uniform stepped out and came directly to Oolooteka. A younger man followed him.

"Chief Jolly." The man of rank had a large bulbous forehead and small piggish eyes.

Oolooteka did not extend his hand in friendship but only nodded.

"Tell Chief Jolly I come with news of the land in the west, the land President Jefferson has offered to the Cherokee," the man said to his aide.

The aide then translated fairly poorly, saying in Cherokee, "Chief Jolly, Colonel Meigs comes with words from the land of the dead."

Oolooteka did not respond—the chief stood tall and dignified, staring ahead.

Clearly impatient, Meigs harassed his aide, asking, "Why do they always take so blasted long to answer? Tell him that young John Ross reports the land is favorable for hunting and farming. I want him to deliver that message to Tahlunteeskee."

Meigs spoke with the peculiar clip of a New Englander. Sam recognized the distinct way of talking, having heard it before when a troupe of Presbyterian ministers from Massachusetts visited Timber Ridge.

After a long pause, Oolooteka answered. In Cherokee, Sam understood the chief to say, "Oolooteka is happy to hear of the bountiful offer of land from our Great White Father Jefferson. Oolooteka asks how the Cherokee would pay for the move as there are no funds for a long journey."

The aide translated it as, "He's happy, but they have no money for travel."

"Well, of course, there'd be consideration." Meigs seemed taken by surprise. Then those pig-eyes landed on Sam. "Where did you come from?"

"Tennessee."

"Don't go stirring up any trouble or taking on the bad habits of these people."

"If living free is stirring up trouble, then it's too late. As for bad habits, from what I've seen, there's plenty on both sides of the border."

Meigs frowned, nodded at Oolooteka, turned his back to them, and marched to the scow. The aide scampered after him like a puppy.

Another week passed, and Sam sat reading under a large oak tree when his brothers James and John appeared. Sam stayed on the ground.

"What are the Holy Apostles doing so far from home?"

"I knew you weren't kidnapped!" John shouted. "Ma couldn't believe you would run off on your own, but I knew better."

Sam set the book down. "How did you find me?"

"A trader said he saw you. We've come to take you back," James announced.

He picked up the book again. "I find I prefer the life here."

James smirked. "You've always been full of your own importance."

"He just can't admit he's a good-for-nothing scoundrel," John said.

Sam jumped to his feet. "Better a free scoundrel than an enslaved repentant." He gave them a dismissive wave of his hand. "Here, I have my liberty and do not suffer under the tyranny of fools like you."

John rushed at him, but Sam easily pushed his brother away. Then he recalled how Oolooteka had treated Colonel Meigs—his dignified and far superior posture, the calm and thoughtful response against the face of an angry and impatient foe. He drew back his shoulders, stood rigid, and stared straight ahead. Sam stood quiet a long, long moment, ignoring the taunts his brothers hurled at him, waiting for their silence, and only then did he speak with a steady voice and no trace of animosity.

Plainly and patiently, he said, "You may be my guardians in Tennessee, but here, you're trespassers and unwelcome guests. I'll come home on my own accord, not yours."

The expression on John's face—shock or confusion—brought a peculiar thought to Sam. Perhaps John needed him around, to steal Sam's successes and make them his own—like taking the beaver skins to the hatter or wanting credit for a deer kill. John must have been aware of his own weaknesses and deficiencies, and the Major wasn't around to make him feel special anymore. Sam envisioned the bleak future that lay ahead for John and could feel only pity for his brother. The feeling passed quickly, and Sam squared his shoulders again. He was his own man now, independent and free to choose his path. As his brothers walked away, Sam wondered what his chosen life would be. All he knew for certain was that his future did not reside at Baker Creek with the Holy Apostles.

Sam heard a rustling of dry leaves behind him but kept his sights on the fat bullfrog. With a fast-handed *whop,* he caught the frog's hind legs.

Little Otter appeared. "Frogs are forbidden before ball play."

For weeks, Sam had heard about the superstitions surrounding the game the Cherokee called *anesta,* loosely understood to mean "little brother of war."

"It's for Howling Nancy."

Sam led the way to her hut. She sat outside, a basket of clams and mussels at her feet. When Sam offered her the frog, the old woman took it from him and immediately slammed the frog's head against a rock.

"The Indian agent comes." Little Otter pointed at a keelboat leaving the garrison across the river.

Around the council fire lately, the men had been asking Oolooteka when the annuity from the United States would be paid. These were monies promised in the treaty signed two years back. The villagers were anxious to receive their share so that they could wager on tomorrow's ball play between the villages of Cayoka and Etowah.

Sam and Little Otter met Oolooteka at his trade store. Colonel Meigs arrived a few minutes later, an aide with him.

After exchanging pleasantries, Meigs said, "Tell Chief Jolly I need a horse to send a man to collect their annuity."

While Little Otter translated for Oolooteka, Sam asked Meigs, "Where's the money?"

It wasn't his concern, but the way the colonel demanded a horse annoyed Sam.

Meigs squinted at him then looked at Oolooteka. "Chief Jolly, the money is in Nashville. If I can borrow a horse…"

Little Otter translated again.

Oolooteka smiled and said in Cherokee, "The agent of the Great White Father should have enough horses to honor his debts to the Cherokee."

Little Otter started to speak, but Sam touched his arm.

"Chief Jolly would like to know why the Indian agent for President Jefferson must beg the use of a village horse to pay the Cherokee."

A red flush formed on Meigs's broad round forehead. He sputtered, "The paddock got left open, and the horses ran off."

The glint in the chief's eye told Sam that Oolooteka had not missed the chagrin on the Colonel's face.

"Their horses escaped," Sam said in Cherokee.

"Tell the Indian agent seven dollars for the use of one of Oolooteka's horses."

Sam hesitated, waiting to see if Little Otter would translate, but his friend seemed to have relinquished the position of linkster to Sam.

"The chief needs seven dollars to rent the horse," Sam told Meigs.

"If I didn't know better, I'd think the chief was a son of Israel," Meigs mumbled.

"Want me to translate that?" Sam asked.

"No, no. Tell him he'll get his money when the deed is done."

A pony was brought out. Meigs and his aide left with the animal. Word quickly spread throughout the village, and the exodus to Cayoka began soon thereafter.

The village of Cayoka had challenged the village of Etowah to a game at the ball ground near Tanisee, fifteen miles upriver. Little Otter would be playing for Cayoka, and Sam had helped with the preparations and training. As far as Sam could tell, only one rule existed in the Cherokee ball play: a player couldn't pick the ball off the ground with their hands but had to use one of their sticks.

Little Otter had shown Sam how to fashion a hickory branch, slender and supple, into the shape of a long spoon with strips of deer hide to form a basket. Sam had gone with Little Otter to collect bat wings, feathers from flycatchers and swallows, and the rattle from a snake. Those items they attached to Little Otter's ball sticks. The bat wings were to give him agility, the feathers would make him swift like the birds that caught insects in flight, and the rattle would frighten his opponent. It sounded childish to Sam, at first. But watching Little Otter and seeing the care and diligence he showed for the preparations gave Sam a newfound respect for Little Otter's reverence for the Cherokee traditions.

Sam spent the last days of summer with Little Otter on the flat ground near the eastern slough, where they practiced playing the game. Running and scrambling to catch the palm-sized ball with their sticks in flight or scooping it off the ground, they had great fun. After a few weeks, Sam was as adept as Little Otter with the ball sticks.

Before they left Hiwassee Island, Little Otter told Sam, "Etowah has many more players over Cayoka. Tooqua Jack will ask Kalunah to play."

The idea that Sam might play startled him. He hadn't been adhering to the rules or making preparations. Also, he'd heard about fasting and secret bloodletting and something about "going to water" before the game. He thought back over the past week, trying to remember if he had eaten a frog or a rabbit. He didn't worry about the rule that forbade touching a woman. Sam simply wouldn't have been with a girl because young Cherokee girls were watched closely by their families.

Little Otter and Sam left for Cayoka by crossing the southern channel, which was shallow after the dry summer months. The path took them up gravelly hills, out of sight of the river. The colors of autumn covered the land. The wind was pleasant, the air crisp and clear. They passed fields recently harvested, where horses grazed in a meadow near a two-story dogtrot like the family home at Baker Creek. Sam thought of his mother and wondered what she would think of him now as he prepared to don a breechcloth and submit to the practice of scratching one's skin with sharpened turkey bones.

They arrived midafternoon at the Cayoka village. Sam had never been that close to the eastern mountains. They appeared like giants peeking over the horizon. The village was similar to the one on Hiwassee Island, if not bigger. Little Otter had a sister there. Instead of seeing her right away, Little Otter went straight to the village shaman, Tooqua Jack.

The old man's head was completely bare save one snatch of hair at the crown, where eagle feathers protruded straight up. Lines of red paint crossed his wrinkled cheeks, and black was smudged under his cloudy eyes. He wore a buckskin tunic with elaborate beading on the fringe. The shaman rose to his feet with some difficulty.

When he saw Sam, Tooqua Jack said, *"Sa go ni ge,"* and brought a finger to his eye.

In English, Little Otter told Sam, "Blue is the color of defeat. He doesn't want to offend the red spirits of victory with your eyes."

Sam answered in Cherokee, "Kalunah's blood is red." That was the best he could think of.

"Kalunah fast like the deer," Little Otter proclaimed in Cherokee.

Another man came forward. *"Kuntee ada-lee i usdi."*

Sam understood he was saying someone named Kuntee had a wife with a baby. He didn't know why that mattered, but like not eating rabbits and collecting bat wings, it must have been another superstition. The rules of Cherokee ball play might be simple, but the customs that preceded the game were not.

The tall, muscular man eyed Sam. *"Kalunah taki-yati Gaska-ya."*

The only word Sam understood for sure was his name.

Little Otter told Sam, "Angry Worm wants to race you."

The shaman nodded, and they cleared a space.

Sam went to stand next to Angry Worm. He buried his head against the wind and ran as hard as he could, keeping pace with Angry Worm for a quarter mile. The shaman seemed unimpressed.

Angry Worm said in Cherokee, "Let us see if Kalunah can capture the ball like the swift catches the fly."

When the shaman tossed a ball in the air, Sam handily trapped it between his sticks.

Angry Worm and Little Otter exhorted the shaman to include Sam in the game. The old man relented only after Sam swore he'd not eaten either frogs or rabbits lately. The moment he proclaimed his abstinence, Sam worried that maybe it hadn't been long enough. He might become timid like the rabbit and lose his courage. The same with a frog—he might have absorbed the brittleness of their bones, causing him to break a leg and become a cripple. He pushed those thoughts aside when the shaman declared Sam would be a provisional player. Tooqua Jack would have the final say the next day.

A messenger was sent to retrieve Kuntee's breechcloth and belt for Sam to wear. Sam's ball sticks were taken, along with Little Otter's, and hung on a tall frame near the banks of the Ocee River. The frame consisted of two forked poles with a crossbeam. The sticks already hanging were decorated with ornaments and charms like Little Otter had done. Sam's sticks were plain and looked quite pitiful, and he questioned if he was really prepared to play. Nobody had said anything about the scratching to draw blood. Maybe he'd misunderstood.

Oolooteka arrived with his wife and daughter and some of the older villagers, like Howling Nancy. A man, swarthy and stout, went to greet Oolooteka. The two men clasped each other by the forearm. Sam had learned this was the Cherokee handshake that meant true and lasting friendship. This must be Tahlunteeskee—*The Upsetter*, chief of Cayoka village and Oolooteka's older brother.

Oolooteka gave notice to Sam. He told his brother, *"Kalunah u-way-chi ah-to-yas-nahi."*

Adopted Son? Did I hear that right?

Tahlunteeskee nodded to Sam. Immediately, Sam sensed Tahlunteeskee was a man of stature not loved easily and freely by his people, like Oolooteka. Rather, Tahlunteeskee commanded respect and fear. Sam could see the true nature of their relationship: Oolooteka would always be second in importance compared to Tahlunteeskee—not too dissimilar to Sam's place in his family, always the afterthought son.

Sam ate a meal of venison jerky and corn porridge with Oolooteka's family while Little Otter went to visit his sister.

Dusk came on suddenly, and Little Otter took Sam to join the other players near a secluded inlet downriver. The shaman was present, with several others there to act as his assistants. Sam stripped like the others, and one of the assistants helped him loop Kuntee's long red breechcloth between his legs, tucking the fabric over the heavily beaded belt then tying the loose ends at the groin, making a snug hold for his privates. Kuntee's belt had a deer tail fastened to it and a snake rattle attached to the band Sam tied across his forehead. Sam's beard had started growing in, which set him apart from most of the other players. The assistants came around with red paint and covered the players' hands and feet. Then charcoal was used to draw black lines around their calves and forearms and mark each of their shoulders with an inverted semicircle and a dot underneath.

The shaman stuck a white-tipped falcon feather onto the headband Sam wore. Sam took this as the sign he'd been accepted to play the next day.

Dressed as though ready for the game, the thirteen players

assembled near the frame holding their sticks. A large fire crackled and spat, and flames leapt into the treetops that overhung the soft level ground selected for the dance. Vines grew in the leafy canopy, casting shadows that swayed in the cool night air. Nature could not have provided a more fantastical stage.

Spectators began to sprawl on the ground or lean against trees. Smaller fires illuminated the edges of the stage. Soon, more Cherokee were gathered there than Sam had ever seen. He felt glad to be a ball player, happy to be in the limelight, to have a purpose and a place. Otherwise, he might have been lost in the crowd.

Meanwhile, a man with a drum sat down near the frame holding the ball sticks. His back was to the players. Seven women formed a line between the drummer and the players. All the women were dressed in light-colored tunics, their hair coiled in buns at the back of their heads, red and white ribbons streaming down over their shoulders.

Then one of the men who had assisted the shaman came and took the ball sticks off the frame, distributing them to the players. Sam held his ball sticks close to his chest like the others. Another man shook a large gourd rattle while he trotted around the players, causing them to form a tight circle. They moved counterclockwise in a simple stomping shuffle. The rattler shook slowly at first then gained speed until he called out, *"Hi!"*

The players responded, shouting *"Hi-hee!"*

The rattler called out, *"Ehu!"*

The players chanted, *"Ha-hee ehu ha-hee ehu,"* in unison, moving faster to keep pace with the rattler. The refrain went on, quicker and louder, until the rattler yelled, *"Ahiye!"*

The players stopped and came together, lifting their ball sticks and touching them all together with a clatter. Quickly, each man spun in place and pretended to toss an imaginary ball with their sticks. Mimicking what the others were doing wasn't hard, but he was taken by surprise when they suddenly all rushed at the women. But they stopped short of touching the women, and the crowd of spectators called out, *"Hu-u."* That seemed to end the first part of the dance.

The man who had distributed the ball sticks took them away and placed them on the frame again. The drummer tapped out a slow, steady beat next. He began to sing, and the women danced in a line, advancing toward the players then wheeling about and moving away, all the while singing a chorus to the drummer's song. Sam tried to make out the meaning of the song. It was all about the next day's game, about winning a horse, a fine stallion, a beautiful pacer, about the defeat of their rivals and the joy of receiving the esteem of their friends.

The women shuffled to and fro, solemn faced, not a smile on their lips as they repeated the refrain *"Hi gan uyahi"* over and over again. At some point, a man ran past the frame where the ball sticks hung, out to the edge of the clearing. He cupped his hands around his mouth and gave out a loud yelp that sounded like a woodpecker tapping a dead tree. Four times he made the peculiar call, the last being a prolonged quaver that the players answered with a chorus of barks and yowls.

Then the man cried out, *"Atsi-tio-klosa!"*

"Etowah has already been beaten!" was the meaning.

The players chanted the phrase loudly, forming two lines and dancing to and fro like the women, only in a different direction. Soon, one of the assistants came and led the players away while the women kept singing and dancing.

The shaman waited at the shore in the same inlet, the river lapping at the soft, sandy bank. For the next while, Tooqua Jack prayed out loud to the Red Hawk and the Red Deer. Then the players drank from the river, and a sour concoction was passed around in a gourd. They walked back to the dance, and that time, Sam noticed a different set of women dancers was there. One of the women, a younger girl, seemed to have a smile on her lips when her eyes met Sam's. Maybe it was his imagination, or maybe the pretty young girl was trying to be friendly.

The ball sticks were distributed again, and the players' dance started up. The ritual preparation for the tournament went on like this for hours—stomping and singing to the measured beat of the drum or the rattle, interrupted at intervals by the woodpecker call, and the players were again taken to the river, where they drank water and the sour concoction that revived Sam's energy.

Like a long dreamlike state, the dance seemed to carry its own special logic. At some point, Sam fell under its spell, feeling the drumbeat reverberate through his body. The dance took hold, and

Sam moved with a force he didn't understand and couldn't resist. Just before sunrise, the rattler threw green pine tops onto the fire, and smoke enveloped the players, and the dancing stopped.

After that, Sam, like the others, returned to his regular clothes. At dawn, Tooqua Jack led them along the path to the ball ground in Tanisee several miles away. Before they reached the ball ground, Tooqua Jack took them to the river. Hidden by laurel bushes, Sam stripped naked and stood with the others in a line, stoically facing the river. An attendant came to him with a comb-like implement made of turkey bone. The implement gave Sam a fright, not so much for fear of the pain but fear of showing weakness in front of the others. He steeled himself as the tool with seven sharpened turkey bones was pressed into Sam's shoulder. It stung as the implement gouged his skin on the downward path to his elbow. Pinpricks of blood formed. Sam looked over at Little Otter. They shared a brave smile as each withstood four sweeps down their upper arms then four more down each forearm and another four on their thighs and calves.

By the time the attendant reached Sam's legs, tiny lines of blood were dripping off his arms. But the sharp pricks felt welcome in a weird way, as though he was earning his right to play. Then the players were led into the water, where the blood washed away. After that, they dressed in their breechcloths, and the attendants came around with charcoal. An X was drawn across Sam's chest and stripes around his arms and legs. After that, Tooqua Jack gave a rousing talk about the opposing players, assigning each of the Cayoka players a specific Etowah rival. Sam was given Long Tail as his personal opponent. The shaman then drew an image of the ball field in the sand. He placed a stake to mark each player's starting position.

Holding his sticks to his breast as the others did, Sam marched single file behind Little Otter to the ball ground. The area selected for the game was a wide strip of bottomland ringed by trees. Goal posts stood about three hundred yards apart. No other lines or borders or boundaries existed, just two goal posts in an open field.

The players stood in position with their ball sticks held out. Then women, old and young, came and draped a piece of calico or a blanket over the sticks as wagers on the game. Wives, sisters, mothers, aunts, and daughters surrounded the other players. Sam felt lonesome and excluded, singled out by being overlooked. He wondered why none of the women he knew on Hiwassee Island came to him. Sensitive to his foreignness, he was feeling a little vulnerable until a young Cherokee girl, the same one he'd noticed during the dance, came forward and placed a long red ribbon across his ball stick. Sam almost said something to her, but he hesitated, unsure if any superstition existed against talking to a woman.

As soon as they heard the sound of the opposing players, an attendant came and collected the wagered goods. The line of Etowah men in yellow breechcloths brought a surge of excitement to Sam. Long Tail was easy to pick out. He wore a belt with a stiff train of horsehair that did indeed look like a tail. He had a thick neck and thicker arms. Sam felt a knot of terror in his empty stomach. After the Etowah players were in position, the rival players hurled threats and taunts across the field until an ancient-looking man walked slowly to the center. He called out to the players, "The Sun is looking down upon you. Play this game as your fathers before you have done. Above all, keep your tempers so that none may say that you got angry or quarreled and that, after it is over, each man may return in peace along the white trail to rest in his white house."

He raised an arm with the ball in his fist. *"Ha! Taldu-gwu!"*—"Now for the twelve!"

The old man tossed the ball into the air. Instantly, everyone dashed to catch it.

An Etowah player had it first. Angry Worm tackled him and threw him to the ground. The ball was loose again. Little Otter scooped it up with his sticks and ran for the rival's goal posts. The Etowah players tossed their sticks to the ground to chase after Little Otter. The Cayoka players dropped their sticks too and tried to tackle the Etowah players.

Little Otter made the first goal. The players collected their sticks and got in position for the next ball toss. That time, Angry Worm caught the ball. The Etowah players fell on him with a fury. As Sam moved to protect Angry Worm, he felt someone grab him by the waist and literally toss him to the earth like a toy thrown in a tantrum, which took all the breath out of him. From the ground, he could see the scramble for the ball up close. Angry Worm lay flat out on the ground too. Sam saw an Etowah player stomp on Angry Worm's shoulder, and the ball rolled away. Long Tail grabbed the ball up with his hand.

"Uwadi guti!" the Cayoka players called out—"With the hand!"

Play was halted, but Angry Worm couldn't get up. The Cayoka assistants pulled him off the field. Time was spent by the Etowah players deciding who on their side would have to leave to keep the players evenly matched. Sam hoped Long Tail would be the one forced to retire, but it was a different player.

The ferocity and physical exertion were well beyond the game that Sam had learned on Hiwassee Island. Young men like Little Otter became ruthless warriors, and the experienced players became tyrants with no mercy for their rivals. At times, two opponents would be strangling each other, and the drivers would take whips to their backs to break up the fight.

By late afternoon, the score held even with eleven goals for each side. Exhausted but possessed by the thrill of the competition, Sam caught the ball in his sticks with the next toss. The Etowah pack descended upon him. He sprinted for the goal posts, a hundred yards away. Beating his feet on the ground, he strained to go faster as he felt opponents gaining on him. Someone jumped on his back, and Sam tumbled to the ground. Stars in his eyes, he remained disoriented for a moment, until the fists flying at him brought Sam around. He fought back, losing sight of the ball. He felt the whip of the driver and untangled himself from Long Tail's grasp. Sam escaped in time to see Little Otter score the twelfth goal for Cayoka.

Physically spent and starving but surprisingly alert, Sam walked with the others down to the riverbank again. Tooqua Jack had stayed there the entire game, working his magic to assure their win. The shaman led the players through a ceremony of victory, urging them to cast aside any animosities and ignore the vengeful carping by the losing rivals. Sam then dressed in his pants and calico shirt. As he went to eat with the others, he noticed the pretty young Cherokee girl again as she walked toward him. He smiled and turned to approach her, but an older woman intercepted them and pulled the girl away.

Sam found Oolooteka with a group of men including Tahlunteeskee. He sat on the ground next to Oolooteka. They drank corn soup from gourd bowls and chewed on venison and ate rabbit stew. Sam was praised for his skills in surviving Long Tail. He learned that Long Tail was a Choctaw, kidnapped as a boy and reared by the Cherokee.

Tahlunteeskee had wagered heavily but seemed unconcerned with the amount he'd won, the same as Little Otter. They didn't appear interested in money or material possessions. The Cherokee simply enjoyed the experience of defeating the other players. Mostly, they were grateful to Tooqua Jack for providing the correct rituals and his ability to coax the spirits to work against their rivals.

The talk then moved to a problem with a white family encroaching into Cherokee territory near Tellico. Despite the last treaty boundaries, white settlers were ignoring the agreement. Sam tried to follow the discussion, but he couldn't fight his exhaustion any longer. Between snatches of sleep, or maybe in a dream, he kept hearing talk of the Mississippi Territory, of selling land and moving west, and someone said, "At least we'll get something for our land rather than just letting the whites steal it like they do."

The next day, while he and Oolooteka made their way back to Hiwassee Island, Sam asked, "Will Oolooteka move to the Mississippi Territory?"

Oolooteka didn't answer immediately. Sam had learned to be patient, to wait for Oolooteka to form his thoughts.

"Tahlunteeskee wrote to the Great Father Jefferson about land on the Arkansas River."

"Why?" Sam asked, incredulous that anyone would want to leave the paradise he'd only recently discovered.

"When the Council learned of Doublehead's treachery, they sanctioned his punishment."

"What treachery?" Sam remembered some of what French Moran had said, but he wanted to learn more, and from a Cherokee.

"Doublehead sold our hunting grounds to the Great White Father. He received land on the Clinch River. My brother has a prosperous tollgate on the land he received in the same agreement. Tahlunteeskee doesn't want to suffer the same fate as our uncle."

"Doublehead was your uncle?"

Oolooteka nodded.

In his wildest imagination, Sam could never have dreamed he would end up becoming the adopted son of Doublehead's nephew!

"Did he really eat the flesh of those men in Kentucky?"

"Yes. My brother, The Bench, was with him."

What a strange family. If Oolooteka could fit in with a savage like his uncle, Doublehead, Sam could surely find his destiny with the Cherokee.

Chapter Six

Sam and Oolooteka rode ponies that had been fed well on the seventy-mile journey to Ustinali. A leisurely weeklong trip through the Chickamauga Valley took Sam through a wondrous place with its verdant enclaves of fertile fields and scattered woods in the surrounding hills. At that time of year, the flowering trees in the undergrowth—pear, peach, and plum—were covered in blossoms of white, pink, and purple. Along the way, there had been persistent pressure to stay a while with each Cherokee family they passed. At the beginning, Sam thought that was simply the Cherokees' natural hospitality. But then he came to realize everyone was eager to hear the news about Tahlunteeskee moving out west. In fact, Tahlunteeskee's absence was the very reason for their trip to Ustinali.

Back when the Bone Moon was full and high in the night sky, Tahlunteeskee and the villagers from Cayoka departed in canoes and flatboats for their new land in the Mississippi Territory. Not long thereafter, a messenger came to tell Oolooteka a grand council would convene in Ustinali when the Flower Moon was half full. With his brother gone, Oolooteka was needed for a momentous vote—whether to abolish the Cherokee Blood Law.

"Sam!" someone called from a distance.

He wondered how much time had passed since he'd heard his given name. Having lost track of the precise English calendar, his only measure of time was the moon, the seasons, and his own body. The feathery spray of chestnut hair peeking from the top of his calico shirt, along with the full beard on his face, proved he was seventeen.

"Sam!" the person called again.

Are they really calling for me? Everyone in Cherokee Territory knew him as Kalunah. He rose up in his saddle and searched the area. As he looked to the south, he spied French Moran waving. The large man stood where a group of traders had gathered at the edge of the small village. Sam waved back, in no hurry to talk.

While he lived on Hiwassee Island, Oolooteka's easy and purposeful ways had rubbed off on Sam. His adoptive father never got angry or excited or did anything in haste. Oolooteka accomplished things without the fuss and impatience so common in the white world. After they dismounted and took the horses to water at the Coosawattee River, Sam left Oolooteka and walked toward the traders' wagons. Old Ned and the same weary nags were with Moran, but wooden casks had replaced the ginseng in the wagon bed.

"Your mother's been asking about you."

"When did you see her last?"

"Why, I saw the good woman a month or so ago at her store."

"Is she well?"

"Yes, but she's worried for you. I told her you're with Jolly's band and your stature with the Cherokee is high. They say you are an honest and faithful linkster."

That was true. Colonel Meigs had made promises of provisions and passports to Tahlunteeskee. But securing what was needed to make the journey out west had taken weeks of negotiations with Sam translating for Oolooteka's brother.

Moran held a tin cup under the cask, turned the spigot, and offered Sam a taste. The rum did violent work against his tongue, burning down his throat, but then it warmed him.

"You've made a bit of a name for yourself after the ball play in Tanisee. I didn't tell your mother about that." Moran winked at Sam. "Will Jolly vote to abolish the Blood Law?" he asked.

The Blood Law was the ancient Cherokee practice of settling feuds. A lot of talk had been going on about it around the council fire on Hiwassee Island.

Moran licked his lips. "How do you like the rum?"

"It's good." Sam gave the cup back to Moran. "But I can't pay you."

"Take a little more."

Sam took another drink, not feeling the burn so much, but definitely the pleasant warmth.

"Tell John Jolly that French Moran can make a fair trade." Moran patted the wooden cask.

Oolooteka didn't trade in rum or other spirits. Moran was trying to use Sam to get to Oolooteka. Disgusted, Sam took his leave quickly. Near the Council House, he found Oolooteka with another man and a boy who looked a few years younger than Sam. The man was speaking angrily to Oolooteka.

"Tahlunteeskee betrayed the Cherokee by leaving our homeland. Your brother didn't consider that the treacherous white man would take our land to compensate for the land Tahlunteeskee receives in Arkansas."

The man stomped off, and the boy followed.

"Who was that?"

"My son and his uncle."

Oolooteka had never talked about having a son, so Sam thought maybe he'd misunderstood. "Why doesn't he live with you?" he asked.

"Boys are raised by the mother's family. It is the Cherokee way. Rattling Gourd thinks Oolooteka has adopted too many habits of the whites. He doesn't like the trading post or that Oolooteka hasn't taken up the war drum. He won't let Crying Bear visit because Oolooteka keeps cats on the island."

"Where do they live?"

"Frogtown. Come, Kalunah will help Oolooteka dress for the council."

After washing in the Coosawattee, Oolooteka unwrapped the deerskin package he'd carried from Hiwassee Island, releasing a strong scent of cedar and sage. The first item removed was an elaborate sort of knapsack.

Oolooteka held it with reverence. "My grandmother made fine work."

The mention of family made Sam want to ask more about the son, but he'd learned that waiting was wiser, for the Cherokee believed an impatient man was a weak man. His adoptive father would tell the story in time. Sam lifted the knapsack, surprised at the weight in his palm. He touched the intricate beadwork, lightly running his fingertips over a swirl of red and white beads stitched into a dark cotton liner. The design ended with the flourish of a curling pigtail, the last bead sewn vertically, as though the tip of the tail was rising up.

Oolooteka laid out the other articles side by side. The belt had similar beadwork. The leggings were red-dyed deerskin, side-seamed with black leather lacing. The long rectangular breechclout was older, made of more red-dyed deerskins.

Oolooteka secured the ornate belt around his waist then placed the long stretch of deerskin between his legs, draping the flaps over the belt. He evened out the flap in the front to fully display the sinew and quills embroidered with red and white beads. Sam helped Oolooteka with the back flap. Then Oolooteka stepped into the leggings and attached the lacing to the belt on either side. Sam knelt down and tied the garters—smaller, thinner versions of the belt— just below Oolooteka's knee.

An ornate tunic completed the costume. Oolooteka looked grand and elegant. A deep feeling of love and admiration and contentment swept through Sam. He felt closer to that man than he ever had to his own father. He couldn't help comparing Oolooteka to his father, although the Major's face and appearance had become harder to bring to mind. That didn't matter anyway. Sam knew what his father would have thought of Oolooteka's heathen dress.

Together, they approached the council house, and Sam began to feel the want of better clothes. He was wearing the same pants and calico shirt he'd left Maryville with the previous year. Oolooteka kept walking while Sam remained by the entrance. A large assembly of people was inside, many dressed in their finest, but others were as poorly attired as Sam.

Sam's experience with the council had been mostly on Hiwassee Island. At night, around the communal fire, the petty conflicts of everyday village life had been resolved by Oolooteka without much formality. The council house in Ustinali was larger than any others he'd seen. It had a circular form, and a fire smoldered in the center. Seven large chairs were positioned in a wide circle. Tall poles held the roof aloft, and three stacks of benches, like berths, lined the walls. The benches were in seven sections, one for each of the Cherokee clans.

He recognized two of the older chiefs, Black Fox and the Glass. Both had visited Hiwassee Island. They sat in special chairs reserved for the principal chiefs representing their clans. Oolooteka sat behind the Glass in the berths reserved for the Red Paint Clan. On the trip to Ustinali, Sam had learned about the other chiefs coming to the grand council. As they took their places, appearing to move in a certain order, Sam tried to match each with the description he'd heard.

Toutcheelengh, from Willstown, wore a cape covered with feathers to represent the Bird Clan. Rising Fawn from the Blue Clan had on a vibrant indigo-dyed frock with heavy fringe. The Ridge came wearing a long cloak of deerskins and a shiny silver gorget on his throat. For the Wild Potato Clan, Pathkiller wore yellow leggings, a red turban, and large silver hoops pierced through his earlobes. Turtle-at-Home had on a wolf skin sewn with streamers that reached almost to the ground.

Sam studied the people in the back benches. Crying Bear sat next to Rattling Gourd with the Deer Clan. The boy was shorter in stature but showed some of the qualities of Oolooteka—a firm mouth and a slight wave to his dark-brown hair. Crying Bear was caught between his uncle and his father. Sam felt sorry for him because Crying Bear was missing out on having the best father Sam had ever known. Feeling a little guilty for taking Crying Bear's place, Sam was nonetheless pleased to have Oolooteka all to himself.

Black Fox rose and moved to address the assembly. He was of ordinary stature and didn't possess the vitality of the younger chiefs. His long black hair had flecks of gray and fell across his shoulders. Earlier, Sam had seen him near French Moran's wagon. The old chief looked about the same age as Sam's father was when the Major died.

Black Fox stood in silence for a while, then in a deep voice, he began to speak. "Of all the wars, none is so dreadful as those of our own people. All former animosities are buried in the ground. We must regard each other as brethren, having the same interests."

He stood for a while longer then returned to his chair.

The next chief to address the council was Pathkiller. Despite the costume, he had a regal stature. In another setting, he could have been a king.

"Remember the words of your late Beloved Man. Although he is gone, there remains behind him ample traces of what he has done for you. He told us to look to the Sun so that we would never be lost."

Sam didn't understand what Pathkiller's words meant, but he didn't have long to ponder them because the Glass stood next. He was a tall, robust man with geometric tattoos on his chest and neck. His red leggings were similar to Oolooteka's, but tied around his waist was a streamer that held a dozen shriveled scalps.

"The Glass wonders how our young sons will become men if there's no warpath to follow, no chase for deer. Will they be more like the white man every day, spending their days without glory in trading houses and tilling the soil like women?"

Then Rising Fawn rose. He had a nose ring, and his earlobes were stretched almost to his shoulders by brooch-sized pendants dangling from each ear.

"There is peace with our neighbors, but Rising Fawn sees that as our people raise great herds of cattle and hogs and have our women manufacture cloth, the whites still want our land. If the Cherokee were to comply with all their requests, we would soon have nowhere to raise our own corn, cattle, or anything else."

Rising Fawn had spoken the truth, and Sam worried how the Cherokee could keep the whites from taking more and more of the land.

Next, the Ridge walked to the center. A fierce-looking man with a large head, thick brown hair, and a deep furrow between his brows, when he spoke, his voice was powerful and sonorous.

"At the last council, we agreed that when blood should be spilled between the clans, the Nation will would now be called to account and to punish the transgressors."

The silence deepened as the Ridge paused.

"In the past, when a man was killed by accident, or murder, his clan would avenge his injuries. In their zeal for revenge, more bloodshed, sometimes against an innocent man, was sacrificed. And if the murderer fled, a clansman was frequently killed in his stead. Too many a good man of our people has died under the blood law."

The Ridge's words were bold and striking, and they carried a message of urgency and change. The others who followed didn't command the same attention, so Sam occupied his hands by whittling a walnut shell to resemble a small open-weave basket. Listening to the different dialects, Sam drifted off into his own imagination until he heard Oolooteka's voice. Then he put his knife aside and drew his attention to his adoptive father. Oolooteka wore no silver trinkets, and his appearance, which had seemed so princely earlier, paled when compared to the principal chiefs. But the slow, smooth cadence of Oolooteka's voice filled the council house.

"If the Cherokee have suffered from the discovery of white men, they have also gained by the superior knowledge they have thereby acquired."

Sam looked around the room, and the other chiefs appeared to be listening intently.

"If we have suffered in war with the Americans, it has taught the Cherokee to appreciate their own people. The Cherokee have come together in the spirit of a unified nation instead of the blinding fury attended with every petty grievance, burning for each other's destruction."

Oolooteka returned to his bench, and a succession of the lesser chiefs came forward to have their say. Sam waited for Rattling Gourd to address the assembly, especially after the heated words about Tahlonteeskee, but he stayed on the bench. Late in the afternoon, the council broke to prepare for the Eagle Tail Dance. The music started, and the old warriors came off the benches individually, taking turns to act out the feats they had performed on the warpath. Those of middle age told of the more recent war with the Americans. The best was a large, rough-hewn man wearing a gorget and silver rings in his earlobes and an eagle's tail feather in his hair.

His name was Big Acorn, and he acted out his story, every motion indicating a sudden and unexpected attack. Crouching down low and with a pretend rifle in hand, his eyes bore down on an invisible foe. He raised the rifle and fired. Shouting the war whoop, he leapt up with the swift action of a panther, attacking the enemy. Then Big Acorn called out to some of the older warriors in the audience, laughing and seeming to mock the ones who had been at the scene, calling them fearful and cautious when Big Acorn had been brave.

His performance continued as he advanced again. That time, Big Acorn held an invisible tomahawk in one hand and an invisible rifle in the other. He motioned for others to follow his lead as he fired, reloaded, and fired again. He pretended to throw the rifle to the ground before racing toward the enemy, stabbing the air with his tomahawk and screaming a ferocious victory whoop. Then he collapsed to the ground, grabbing at his knee as though injured, only to rise again to fight off another foe until his leg gave out. He pretended to limp, still firing his rifle, commanding the others to pursue the enemy with vigor.

Oh, if only I could have been in battle with Big Acorn… What an adventure that might have been!

The Eagle Tail dance ended long after midnight. The next day, the council reconvened and voted to abolish the Blood Law. They also voted to deny the Americans' request for access to the Coosa River.

Another dance took place that night. The women dancers with their chickicoos—turtle shells with pebbles inside—fastened to their knees kept time with the drumbeats. They moved in a wide circle, then an older woman dragged The Glass into the center. The Glass staggered and could hardly stay on his feet. He was among those who'd visited the wagons with barrels of whiskey and rum.

Someone produced a fiddle, and all the women, especially the young girls, began to pick partners. A pretty girl in a red-and-white calico dress walked toward Sam. It was the same girl from the ball play in Tanisee, the one who had placed a ribbon on his ball stick. She had smooth tawny skin with coal-black hair and dark-brown eyes.

After their first dance together, Sam asked, *"Ga-do de-tsa-do-a?"*

She shook her head. "I don't speak Cherokee. A kind white family raised me, but I was returned to my aunt last summer." She spoke English with no deficiency or accent.

Sam took her hand. "What is your name?"

"They called me Patsy in Virginia."

Sam caught his breath, and his pulse beat furiously as though someone was skipping stones with his heart. A wave of pleasure flooded his body. *Is this the invisible hand of God or the Great Spirit?* He didn't know how else to explain the improbable luck of meeting a beautiful Cherokee girl who knew both the world Sam came from and the world he wanted to be part of. It couldn't be chance—it had to be Fate.

"My aunt calls me…" Patsy fumbled with the word. *"Awee… awee-*

acto. Something that sounds like that."

"*Awi-akta,*" Sam said. "It means Doe's Eyes."

Patsy smiled at him. Sam gave her the tiny walnut-seed basket he'd whittled. The fiddle started up again. Sam took Patsy's hand, his other arm around her waist, and they did a sort of lively promenade among the other dancers. They moved together as one, and thoughts of kissing her filled Sam's head. His heart fluttered with joy, and his mind raced with excitement about the future. Patsy had to be the one. Their meeting couldn't have been a coincidence. It had to be fate. He could see them as man and wife—there or out west or even at Baker Creek. Maybe Sam could return to Virginia with Patsy as his wife.

They danced together as though in a delightful dream. Patsy in his arms felt like a hand fitting a glove. It went on like that until someone grabbed Sam's arm. He turned to find a short, older, full-blooded Cherokee woman with pockmarked cheeks clutching him. The old woman spat at Sam's feet and shouted, *"A-sga'si-ti!"*—"Dreadful!"

That was the worst insult a Cherokee could think of. They had no other words for profanity.

The woman yanked Patsy away from Sam. *"Usga'seti."*

"What does she say?" Patsy asked him.

"I'm a bad young man," he muttered.

Then a Cherokee man joined her, saying, "His clothes are insulting."

"He has no cow or farm." The old woman came closer to Sam. "The Cherokee only tolerate you. You don't belong here."

The words stung, and Sam felt the pressure of everyone's eyes on his shabby appearance. He dropped his head and left the dance. He wandered aimlessly along the river, numb from the torrent of emotions brought on by the old woman's rebuke. Under the light of a waxing half-moon, Sam found a trail leading up a hill to the north. Soon, dawn approached, and swords of blinding white light cut through the gray clouds hovering over the peaks in the east. The sun rose over the ridge, and the morning light cast the valley before him into a darkness deeper than night. A desire to see Ma brought water to his eyes. He missed Paxton and his sisters. He even missed Granny Peg. Even the animosity toward the Holy Apostles had softened, although that was hard to admit.

Time to go home. He walked back to the place where they'd kept the horses. Oolooteka was there, readying for the journey home to Hiwassee Island.

"Kalunah must visit his white family," was all Sam said.

Offering an explanation hardly seemed necessary, and none was asked for.

Sam took up a path that led north. Blinded by the insults slung at him by the old Cherokee woman, he walked under a cloud of despair. The first sight that captured his attention was John Vann's large plantation. Seeing the wealth and evidence of success—the big house, the barns, and servants' quarters—only reinforced his humiliation. The force of disgust the old woman had shown by spitting at his feet was the worst he'd ever seen a Cherokee treat another. She was right, though—his clothes were in tatters, and he didn't have a cow or a farm of his own. The truth of it cut deeply, causing a reckoning with reality in Sam's heart. What a fool he'd been to think he could court a girl like Patsy. She might have been happy with dancing, but she would also expect to be taken care of and given fancy things.

Sam didn't want the farmer's life. Yes, when harvest time came the previous fall, he had joined the Hiwassee Island villagers to pick corn and tobacco, happy to toil alongside the others for the camaraderie. Many times, he helped out in Oolooteka's store. But he did the work willingly, for the pleasure and to show gratitude, not for money. And he'd spent hours translating between Tahlunteeskee and Colonel Meigs, neither expecting any payment nor feeling any obligation. Everything he'd done had been for friendship.

Doubt crept in under the glare of the afternoon sun, causing Sam to fear the old Cherokee woman had spoken the truth when she said he didn't belong with the Cherokee. He thought he'd been accepted, but perhaps he'd been wrong. Maybe everyone had been hospitable simply because he was with Oolooteka.

A few miles on, he came to McNair's Trade Store, and night settled in without Sam noticing. He should have found a convenient place to rest, but the great thrashing about inside his head pushed him on. A gibbous moon, at the zenith of its nightly transit, illuminated the path. He took no notice of other travelers nor worried about horse thieves or any other dangers. A restive uncertainty had taken full possession of his mind, and he wrestled with questions he could neither answer nor put to rest. He'd been convinced he was respected and looked up to in the Cherokee territory, believing he'd won his place in the Nation. He'd thought his performance in the ball play had elevated his stature with the villagers on Hiwassee Island because the men who'd been standoffish at first began to praise him around the council fire. But maybe everything was a delusion and he was indeed only tolerated, as the old woman claimed.

When he reached the Hiwassee River, the moon was dipping low in the west, and Sam walked across the shoals in the early hours of the morning. How different it was from when he'd crossed the Little Tennessee the year before. The whole world had been open to him then. Now, he was scurrying home with his tail between his legs. A slow shift took place, and the doubt about his dignity among the Cherokee was soon replaced by a desire to stall his return to Baker Creek.

Then rain began to fall, and he remembered *i'yah gatu'si*—Pumpkin Hill, a hunting camp that would be empty that time of year. He began to feel hungry, for the only things he'd eaten were the spring greens that grew along the path and the nuts he'd found. He followed the deer traces high into the hills, moving in the general direction he remembered. He reached the small shelter made of logs holding up a bark roof just as the skies opened and rained down a torrent of water. Finally able to sleep, he dreamt of shouting at the old Cherokee woman, trying to defend himself against her insults and taunts.

For days, he lived off rabbit and squirrel, brook trout, sorrel, lamb's quarter, and berries. In the solitude, alone and away from the opinions of others, he examined his feelings and began to see the events at Ustinali, free from the heat of passion and independent of the prejudices of others. The old woman had not spoken for the Cherokee Nation. She didn't know of the valuable service Sam provided as a linkster. She couldn't know that Little Otter was his friend and that Sam helped to care for Howling Nancy. Patsy was the one who'd chosen Sam, not the other way around. He hadn't ever expected the love and respect he felt from Oolooteka. With enough time, Sam purged the melancholy from his mind, if not his heart. One evening, a large waxing moon rose in the east at the time the sun fell behind the mountains to the west. Sam tied a string of rabbit and squirrel skins around his waist and set off for Baker Creek. Some of the desire for home had lessened, and his apprehension grew over how he would be received, whether his mother would welcome or reject him. But he was ready to be at home with his family. The moonlight was a powerful guide as he strode down the eastern slope.

Just before daybreak, as he neared the family farm at Baker Creek, a sense of dread took hold. *Will Ma be angry and cold towards me?* Sam made his way to the small rivulet below the farmhouse. After washing off, he sat for a long while, anxious about the reception he would receive from the family. But Sam had nowhere else to go and was entitled to a share in his father's estate. Mostly, he wanted to see his mother, hoping to feel her love and affection.

He walked slowly out of the wood and approached the house. The family was gathered around a table in the dogtrot breezeway.

"Sam!" His mother's hand flew to her mouth. "I didn't know who you were until I saw your eyes."

Granny Peg was sitting at the table, next to Ma. "He's brown as a berry."

Ma got to her feet and reached for him. Sam went to her. His mother put a hand on his shoulder, and her touch washed all his anxieties away. He put an arm around her and bent his head against her shoulder. They embraced for a long moment. He felt as though he'd never left but, at the same time, that he'd been gone a lifetime.

The family was sharing a plate of ham and bread and milk for their morning meal.

John didn't stop chewing when he said, "You come in looking like a dirty savage. I might have shot you, and I'd have been justified in doing so."

"Shush." Ma turned to Granny Peg. "Fetch a plate for Sam." Then to William, she said, "Bring out another chair."

James pointed at the pelts. "Are those skins?"

"They'll make good moccasins," Sam said.

James scoffed. "For your squaw?"

Polly rose from her chair and came to Sam. She'd matured in the year he'd been gone. Her face no longer bore the chubby cheeks of a child, and the high-waisted frock she wore showed the rounded contours of a young woman. She turned her earnest gray eyes up to him. "Sam, I made a new suit of clothes for you. Ma said you'd need them when you came home."

He smiled and took her hand. "Thank you. I sorely do need a new costume."

"But it isn't a costume. It's trousers and a frock coat."

He chuckled. "Polly, the Cherokee call their clothes costumes."

Granny Peg returned with a plate, and William brought a chair for Sam. He moved to sit next to Paxton.

"Sam, take off the pelts before you come to the table," Ma said.

He dropped the pelts on the wood floor.

"I didn't expect to see you again," Paxton said. "But I'm glad you're home. It's been too quiet since you've been away."

Paxton seemed to have shrunk in size, his skin as pale as ever, and his lips had a bluish tint.

Sam tried not to show his alarm, but his voice quavered when he said, "I wish you had been with me."

Then he caught Eliza staring at him. Sam winked at her and made a face. She looked down for a moment and then snuck a coy glance at him again.

"Where's Robert?" Sam asked.

"He returned to Virginia," Ma said.

Polly stood. "Ma, can I bring out Sam's new suit?"

His mother shook her head. "It can wait."

After the meal was finished, Sam went with Polly to try on his new clothes. She held out a pair of woolen pants for him. "They're in the new fashion. James said it's what the men in Knoxville wear now."

Sam took the trousers from her and held them up to his waist, expecting they'd be too short for him, but they reached all the way to his feet.

"How did you know what length to make them?"

"I left them extra long. Try them on."

Sam turned away from Polly before stepping out of his old pants, worn through at the knees and tattered at the hem. He slipped into the trousers. The pants legs were close-fitting and tapered to his feet. He buttoned the waist flap, feeling the extra room.

Polly bent down on her knees and fastened two buttons on flaps at the ankles. Then she brought the frock coat to him. "Ma let me use extra cloth so I could do the fancy pleating in the back."

She held the coat open, and Sam slid his arms in. The coat fell below his knees and had a stiff collar that almost touched his ears. He wondered what Patsy's family would have thought if he'd worn those clothes in Ustinali. The regret and humiliation swept over him for a moment until he saw Polly's eager face.

"Why, this is the best suit of clothes I have ever owned, Polly." He spun around in a tight circle for her.

She clapped her hands with delight. "Are you going to stay home now? Because I missed you. James and John never notice me, and William isn't much fun."

He hugged her, saying, "I'll stay as long as you want, Polly."

The next morning, Sam woke with a fever and chills as though all the sickness had waited for his return to the safety of Ma's care. Paxton sat with him for most of that period. Sam was too ill to talk, and Paxton's voice was weak, so they communed in silence. Polly brought soup and water, and Ma came often to test his fever, but the others mostly ignored him. Nearly a month passed before Sam regained his strength and energy.

One sunny afternoon, Ma took Sam out to the barn.

"Cousin Matthew sent these for you."

She pointed at a crate in a corner. Inside, Sam found the books they'd left behind in Virginia. He was thrilled to see Livy's *History of Rome*, the geography book with maps of the world, and many others he didn't remember, like the fifteen volumes of the history of England and translations of Tacitus and Thucydides.

When Paxton was too tired to venture beyond the house, which was most of the time, Sam would stay and read aloud while they sat in the breezeway. They couldn't talk like they used to, for their old dream of running off together had silently died and lingered like a ghost that represented the impenetrable divide between them. And Sam couldn't share stories of his time with the Cherokee either, for it only reminded him that he'd abandoned his brother.

As summer reached its peak, in the woods north of the house, Sam built a bark lean-to under a tall white oak. He could read in peace during the day, and if the night was mild, sleep there too. He passed the time exploring his newfound library and renewing the friendships with his cousins. Sam contributed to the farm chores, but other than picking up shot and powder and other supplies of convenience, he avoided the family store in Maryville.

One morning in late September, alone in his bark lean-to, Sam heard footsteps outside.

"Sam!" John yelled.

Sam rolled out, making a show of taking his time getting to his feet. Both his older brothers were glaring at him.

James waved a piece of paper. "You've been taking what you pleased from the store all summer."

"You owe us nineteen dollars and forty-three cents," John said.

"Take it out of my share."

Sam moved to re-enter the lean-to, but John rushed at him, screaming, "Maybe you could get away with loafing around with Oofooluka, but not with us!" John pushed Sam backward.

Sam took a moment before saying, "Oo-loo-te-ka," enunciating the word slowly and clearly. Then he stared straight ahead and kept his silence.

"This Ooloofuka, he isn't concerned for your welfare or your future, not like your guardians are," John said with a sneer.

"Sam is learning every day from his books and the Cherokee." Instantly, he realized he'd lapsed into the Cherokee way of talking.

James came closer. "To do what? Drink whiskey? Steal horses? What could those savages possibly teach you?"

"Sam works in Oolooteka's trading house. He's a good linkster there and at the garrison too."

"They sleep on dirt floors and wear skins," John said. "What kind of future is that?"

"Sam lives well on Hiwassee Island. Oolooteka has a big farm and a large trading house. Oolooteka never went on the warpath. He's half white and more of a gentleman than either of you will ever be." Sam felt emotion welling in his eyes. "You, my brothers, the Holy Apostles, taught me to hate the Cherokee without ever knowing them. Among the sons of the forest, I have found more fellowship and understanding than I ever received from you two."

He turned on his heel and stomped away. Without much thought, he started on the path for Maryville, fuming that his brothers would expect him to pay for his provisions when they could have taken it from his share of their father's estate. The cooling air was brisk, but the sun still held the warmth of summer. As he neared the town, he was drawn to the sound of a distant drumbeat. He followed it to where the local Tennessee Militia was holding a muster on open land opposite the courthouse. It was a rather pitiful affair, compared to his memories of Virginia, except for a cask of cider.

Sam joined a dozen men standing around a captain, a man about thirty, whom Sam recognized as the son from a prominent Maryville family. Captain John B. Cusack seemed to be holding court rather than conducting a military exercise. After an hour or so, some of the more serious soldiers demanded action. The fife and drum played a marching cadence, and Captain Cusack put down his cup of cider to lead the columns. Sam stood in formation with the others, four abreast.

Captain Cusack strutted forward, and the line of men followed, but within a few yards, the formation wobbled and stumbled. Many of the men couldn't walk a straight line. The drum made Sam want to dance. He stomped and moved in a circle while pretending to beat a drum. This broke the formation completely because of laughter from some and condemnation from those with genuine military zeal.

Cusack pointed his sword at Sam. "You, come up here, and take over the drum."

Sam came forward.

"What's your name?"

"Sam Houston, sir."

Cusack told the drummer to give the instrument to Sam.

With the drum strapped on, Sam used his hands to beat a riff from a rhythm he'd heard often at the Cherokee dances. *Boom-bang-boom-bang-rap-rap-rap.*

Cusack grabbed Sam by a shoulder. "Let's have another cup to quench your thirst."

With the drum still strapped on, Sam walked with Cusack to the cask. By then, the muster had been completely abandoned. Once the cask was dry, Sam and Cusack carried the drum over to a tree stump and set it on its side. They each took a drumstick and competed to see who could beat the fastest, loudest, and longest.

Not far away, the sheriff leaned through an open window in the courthouse. "Quit making all that noise. Court is in session."

Cusack picked up the drum and walked nearer the window and, once directly under it, pounded with a fury until the sheriff came outside. Sheriff Robert Houston, a little man built like a bantam cock, was another distant cousin. Sam had heard others say the sheriff had more bluster than brains.

The sheriff waved his arms as he walked toward them. "You are disturbing the court."

"Crack away, Sheriff," Cusack said.

"Cousin Robert," Sam said. "We're just having a little fun."

"It's Sheriff Houston to you. Disrespectful Indian lover."

The sheriff turned toward Cusack. "I expected better of you. What will your father say?"

"He'll be proud that I'm drumming up support for the militia." Cusack laughed and quickly pushed the drum aside to grab the sheriff by the arm. He motioned Sam to take the sheriff's other arm. Together, they lifted the short man off his feet and wheeled him around. The sheriff's legs ran in midair as he struggled against two stronger young men.

Tossing him toward the courthouse steps, Cusack said, "Best let the militia have its muster."

The sheriff stumbled inside. Sam and Cusack returned to the window and beat on the drum a little longer, but with much less fervor because as the cider wore off, so did their amusement.

Sam returned to Baker Creek under a dark, moonless sky. The cold night wind forced him out of his drunken haze. He slept in the barn under a horse blanket he pulled off his crate of books. He didn't wake until near dinnertime the next day. Then he went to the creek, drank heavily of the cool water, and washed his face and neck.

That was his first experience with the aftereffects of too much alcohol. He climbed up to the house and sat in the breezeway. His head pounded, and an empty stomach churned while the events of the previous day crept back in patchy images and fuzzy recollections. His head was in his hands when James walked by, waving a piece of paper. Sam girded himself for a lecture about his debt to the Maryville store, but James passed by without a word.

Inside the house, James yelled, "Ma, come see what the sheriff gave me this morning!"

In a quick minute, Ma was at Sam's side. John and James hovered behind her.

"Sam," she said. "The sheriff says you were causing trouble at the courthouse."

John read aloud from the paper, "Disorderly, riotously, wantonly annoying the court!"

"Is this true?" Ma stared down at him, her lips pulled in and arms crossed tight.

Sam let out a long sigh. "I believe it may be so."

"Have you been drinking?" she asked.

"There was a muster, and they had some refreshments, Ma."

"I told you this would happen!" John shouted. "He learned to drink from those ungodly heathens he calls his family."

Sam raised his head to John. "That's not true. It's Captain Cusack who was free with the cider."

James snatched the paper from John. "The sheriff has fined you five dollars."

John leaned in close to Sam's face, the smell of coffee on his breath. "How are you going to pay that?"

"Shush, you two. I'll talk to Cousin Robert." Ma went inside, leaving Sam with his brothers.

Sam stood slowly, and the blood rushed to his head. Taking a moment to gain his balance, he tried not to show how unsteady and ill he felt. He walked away without a word and went to the kitchen in search of something to settle his stomach. The aroma of stewing collard greens filled the small room, and the nausea returned. Sam dropped onto a stool, resting his head in his hands again.

A loaf of bread was on the table. Granny Peg sliced the heel off and handed it to Sam, saying, "I see you got the Major's weakness."

She turned and gave the coals a quick stir. With her back to him, Granny Peg said, "I don't know what's goin' to happen to you. You'll either be found dead on somebody's doorstep or end up a big governor somewhere. Only the Lord knows, not me." Then she glanced over her shoulder. "But I pray every day for my Elizabeth. Because your ma has had trouble enough—she don't need you bringing more to her. You hear me, Sam?"

If he stayed at Baker Creek, he could see there would only be more trouble. He would never be satisfied working on the farm, not with the way his guardians, the Holy Apostles, treated him. Sam couldn't face Ma right then, so as soon as he felt better, he gathered his possessions, adding to his knapsack the first volume of Thucydides. After securing the crate of books under the blanket, Sam started for the road to Southwest Point. The wind picked up, and leaves fell heavily from the trees—red, russet, yellow, and orange painted the road leading southwest. Hunting season had come, and Sam was eager to return to the Cherokee. But he couldn't show up without gifts for Oolooteka and his family. He went directly to Sheffy's to pick up what he needed, but Mr. Sheffy refused to extend much credit, and Sam was forced to stay on and work off some of the debt.

He bunked in his cousin's storehouse again and found the lively river town diverting at first. But as the New Year approached, the days were slipping away. The Cherokee would be at their hunting camps, and Sam was eager to join the chase with his friends.

Just before the turn of the year, Sam started the forty-mile trek to Hiwassee Island. He departed Southwest Point carrying a bundle filled with needles, thread, beads, calico, ribbons, lace, tin cups, hand mirrors, a whetstone, and blankets as gifts for his Cherokee friends. For himself, he'd purchased shot and powder, a small cache of fishhooks, and a new felt hat. Even after clerking in the store, Sam left owing twelve dollars and thirty-seven cents.

Bearing the gifts and wearing the new suit of clothes Polly had sewn, Sam felt he could return to Hiwassee Island with a degree of respect and dignity after the terrible dressing down he'd received in Ustinali. He rode the ferry across the river and quickly found the footpath that followed the eastern shore of the Tennessee River. A cold, brisk wind blew in from the west. Sam went along unhurried, enjoying the peacefulness of the pristine woodland. He delighted in the chatter of the birds and the squirrels scampering about in the heavy leaf mold. He camped for a night at a sheltered creek and made his plans while stripers roasted on a spit. As long as he had hooks, twine, and a stream full of bass and trout, he could live quite easily, which gave him comfort and confidence in his future.

With a clear head, he considered how much had changed in the last year and a half. He imagined what the year ahead held—perhaps a comfortable life with the Cherokee or travel out west to join Little Otter in the Mississippi Territory. But he didn't know how he could pay for the provisions he'd need. Working for Mr. Sheffy could be a means of supporting himself, but Sam knew the life of a clerk, beholden to every dolt demanding a measure of salt, was a miserable existence.

Savoring the roasted fish, he brushed aside the questions of where and how he could prove he was meant for greater things. On the cusp of turning eighteen, Sam believed in his destiny and felt certain that the mysterious hand of fate would somehow provide a life much bigger and better than being a farmer or store clerk. He truly expected his future would be a bountiful dish.

Chapter Seven

"Howling Nancy will like this."

Sam held up a thin strand of blue ribbon. The gifts he'd bought lay on the floor of Oolooteka's cabin. In the corner, the calico cat nursed a new litter.

Oolooteka said, "Howling Nancy went to the Great Spirit." He motioned for Sam to follow him. They left Oolooteka's wife and daughter with the trinkets.

Oddly, when Sam returned to the island, he found his adoptive father in a pair of woolen pants and a calico shirt under a blanket draped around his shoulders. They walked to the southern slough, where the pigs foraged for acorns in a dense copse of water oaks. Oolooteka pointed at a fresh mound of dirt covered with rocks. Sam assumed it was Howling Nancy's grave, the first time he'd known anyone from the village to die.

"The hogs rooted up an old burial. When Howling Nancy found the bones scattered about, she started to howl again, saying the Great Spirit was angry about the mill."

On his journey from Southwest Point, Sam had noticed a mill operating a mile upriver.

Oolooteka paused, glancing up at a sky covered with clouds of curds and whey.

"We reburied the bones with all the correct rituals and cleansing, but Howling Nancy kept crying that she could hear Mother Earth's bones grinding in the mill. She howled and moaned for days, and then one morning, we found her dead. We placed her bones with her family."

"This isn't her grave?" Sam asked.

"These are the ancient bones the hogs disturbed. A good medicine man from Mouse Creek came and purified the grave. But many in the village believe the Great Spirit remains displeased."

Sam noticed other subtle signs of change on the island. His lean-to had been taken over by a family of possums, and the council fire had nearly doubled in size because the Cayoka families who'd not left with Tahlunteeskee were aligning themselves with Oolooteka. The fire remained an informal affair, allowing even the older women to have their say. A man named Dreadful Water spoke frequently. He appeared to be the same age as Oolooteka but differed greatly in his style and posture. Dreadful Water would strut in front of the fire with his arms bent and elbows pushed back, his fists clenched, while more often than not, he berated the council about the new mill and other signs of white encroachment. Sam suspected Dreadful Water had ambitions to assert himself as equal in stature to Oolooteka. Sam didn't know what Oolooteka thought and didn't ask, not wanting to put words to his fears of a coming power struggle.

One night, Dreadful Water hurried to speak before anyone else.

"Tsali has a message from the Great Spirit. He calls the people to Ustinali to hear his words." His voice carried a proud and haughty tone and seemed disrespectful toward Oolooteka.

"Who is this Tsali?" Sam asked boldly.

Oolooteka stroked the calico cat in his lap. "Tsali is the sorcerer who lives high in the mountains."

"Tsali has great power," Dreadful Water said. "I have seen the ferocious black wolves who attend him wherever he travels."

Oolooteka stayed silent while Dreadful Water harangued the council with the urgency of Tsali's message.

"The Cherokee Nation must hear Tsali's words."

The others debated what Tsali's message could be and who should journey to Ustinali. Oolooteka listened to each and all without comment. The discussion went on for some time, as did the debate within Sam. He wanted to go to Ustinali, hoping Patsy would be there too. He had saved a piece of lace for her. However, another part of him kept reliving the shame and humiliation he'd suffered from her family. He did have better clothes now, which might make a difference. He waited anxiously for Oolooteka to weigh in on the matter.

Before Oolooteka spoke, Dreadful Water announced, "Dreadful Water will lead the journey to Ustinali."

Only then did Oolooteka stand, the cat unceremoniously losing her seat. Sam fully expected his adoptive father to assert his authority. Instead, Oolooteka asked, "Who else will journey with Dreadful Water to bring Tsali's message back to Hiwassee?"

Three others—Bobtail, Little Terrapin, and Gunstocker—rose and moved to stand near Dreadful Water.

Later that night, when they were alone, Sam asked, "Why does Oolooteka not go to hear Tsali's message?"

"Oolooteka does not need to hear bad talk," the chief replied.

In the waning days of winter, Sam spent most of his time sitting outside Oolooteka's trading house, reading. If someone needed a translation, he would be at the ready. Otherwise, he had his nose in a history of the Trojan War, a story teeming with pirates, barbarians, and bitter rivalries across the Aegean Sea. Thucydides' first volume turned out to be the perfect companion to Homer's poem.

Several weeks passed before Dreadful Water and the others returned from Ustinali. That evening, after the villagers gathered around the council fire, Dreadful Water began to tell the story of Tsali's message. He put a hand to his ear and looked up at the sky, proclaiming, "One night, Tsali and his friends heard distant thunder and thought a storm was ready to break. Tsali saw giant warriors riding black horses among the stars. The leader beat a drum, and he came close to Tsali and his friends."

Dreadful Water spoke with great emotion and acted out the part of Tsali by shielding his head to show fear.

"The leader said, 'Do not be afraid. The Great Spirit has sent us. He has withdrawn his protection over the Cherokee because they have adopted the white man's ways. You can see for yourselves— your hunting is gone, and you are planting the corn of the white man. You have mills and plows, tables and feather beds, and wear the clothes of the white man. The worst Cherokees now have books and allow cats in their presence.'"

Sam glanced at the calico sleeping next to Oolooteka.

Then Dreadful Water tilted his head up and cupped a hand behind his ear to show he was listening to the Great Spirit. He shouted, "The Cherokee must return to the ancient ways!"

Dreadful Water returned to his seat. Little Terrapin stood and took Dreadful Water's place. He recited Tsali's words without gestures or emotion.

"Tsali sees the whites are different from the Cherokee. Our people are made of red clay, and the others are from white sand. The Great Spirit's message is to kill your cattle, your hogs, and your cats, cut short your frocks, dress as a warrior. Discard all fashion of the whites, abandon any communication with each other except by word of mouth, give up mills and looms and all the arts learned from white people. If the Cherokee do this, the game will reappear, and the whites will go away."

Little Terrapin paused and used the silence to let his squinted eyes roam over the nervous audience. Then he continued, "The Great Spirit says to believe and obey. If not, the Great Spirit will strike you dead." He ended with a loud clap of his hands.

Next, Bobtail stood before the villagers, his chest pushed high in the air to represent The Ridge, for he was the chief who had spoken at the council after Tsali.

"Tsali's talk will lead to war, and the Cherokee will suffer. It is false. Tsali does not talk for the Great Spirit. I stand here and defy the threat that he who disbelieves shall die. Let the death come upon me. I offer to test this scheme of imposters."

Bobtail strolled proudly before the men, staring at them. Then, without warning, Gunstocker jumped up and rushed at Bobtail, appearing to attack him. Bobtail fought back and overwhelmed Gunstocker. But then Gunstocker seemed ready to kill Bobtail and only stopped when Little Terrapin intervened and pulled Bobtail to safety.

So strange. The Ridge had almost been killed. That rattled Sam to his core because the Ridge was like Hector—righteous, humble, and fearless. A line from the *Iliad* came to him:

"Perhaps great Hector then found his fate,
But Jove and destiny prolong'd his date.
Safe from the darts, the care of heaven he stood,
Amidst alarms, and death, and dust, and blood."

Sam felt as though he was living in a Cherokee version of Homer's poem. He saw how much infighting was occurring within the Nation, no different from the Greeks in Agamemnon's army.

Oolooteka stood and called for calm. "Tomorrow, Oolooteka will kill some beeves to celebrate the message from Ustinali. We shall feast and remain in tranquility." Oolooteka then went on to thank each man—Dreadful Water, Little Terrapin, Bobtail, and Gunstocker—for making the journey.

The feast relieved some of the tension in the village, but just a few days later, Dreadful Water came back to the council fire with a new message from Tsali.

"The Great Spirit has sent word to Tsali. He will be bringing a hailstorm to destroy all the earth except on the highest mountain. Tsali urges the true Cherokee to abandon their homes, farms, cattle, and hogs, even their slaves. They must join him atop the mountain."

Dreadful Water pointed his arm at the sky. "All who do not obey will be destroyed."

Gunstocker stood and proclaimed, "We must follow Tsali, or we will be ruined."

None of the other men stood to speak, and Sam waited anxiously for Oolooteka to respond. After a long silence, Oolooteka stood before the council.

"Oolooteka sees that The Ridge still lives. Oolooteka tastes the berries on the vine and eats fruits from the trees. Soon, the corn will be knee-high. Oolooteka does not wish to leave the land where he prospers and feels the protection of the Great Spirit."

He sat down, and the calico cat climbed into his lap. No one stood after him. The pipe passed around many times in complete silence. Abruptly, Dreadful Water left the council fire. Gunstocker followed him, but the other men appeared to side with Oolooteka, mostly.

Sam needed a fresh supply of shot and powder, so one morning, he set out for Southwest Point, dreading having to spend several weeks working at Sheffy's to pay off his debt. Only a short distance after crossing the channel, he came upon a small Negro boy on the path. At first, the boy tried to hide, but Sam held out a piece of dried venison. The boy took it and ate hungrily.

"Where are you from?" Sam asked.

After some effort, Sam learned the boy came from Gunstocker's farm. He'd been left alone when Gunstocker abandoned his farm as

Tsali had commanded. Sam took the boy back to Hiwassee Island, and soon after, Oolooteka, Sam, and a few other men from the village rode up to Gunstocker's farm. Sam helped to round up the livestock and drive the animals to a place with plenty of feed. The milk cows were taken back to the island. In the bargain, Sam gained the use of a painted pony. A few days later, he started again for Sheffy's but riding, that time. When he reached the turnoff, knowing he needed to work off his debts, Sam still couldn't abide spending the best of summer in a dusty trade house. The luxury of reading when he liked and the prospect of summer dances led him to take the path to Baker Creek instead.

After a visit with his mother and Paxton, who was mostly bedridden, he ate a meal under Granny Peg's scornful eye. He collected more books than he could carry on foot and secured them to the pony. But he couldn't return to the Cherokee empty-handed. He led the pony into Maryville and made a quick round of the local merchants, including the family's store. Careful to incur only a small debt at each place, Sam replenished his stock of shot and powder and bought enough trinkets and items of convenience to please his friends. He returned to Hiwassee Island with Livy's history of Rome.

By the time the corn tassels appeared and the smaller streams began to dry up, the date foretold for the end-of-the-world hailstorm came and went. The Great Spirit did not destroy everything after all. Those Cherokee who'd left for the mountains slowly crept back to their farms, and life seemed to return to its usual rhythm. The pawpaw fruits dropped from the trees, and cicadas filled the air with their incessant buzzing. Sam returned the painted pony to Gunstocker without regret, for he'd fallen in love with the history of the Punic Wars and spent most of his days reading and rereading the epic battles between Rome and Carthage. His favorite was the Battle of Zama, when a face-to-face meeting had Hannibal offering terms but Scipio refusing, demanding unconditional surrender or battle. Once the fight began, Hannibal used eighty elephants to charge the Romans, but Publius Cornelius Scipio outsmarted the animals with loud horns and a feint in the formations. If he wasn't reading, Sam was on flights of fancy, imagining life as if he'd lived in those times.

Then something else strange happened to unsettle the villagers. A bright star appeared in the night sky. Every night, it seemed to glow more brightly, and soon, a long, thin veil of scattered light covered half the sky. It became the central topic of speculation at the council fire. Perhaps it was another message from the Great Spirit. Nobody knew what it meant.

Summer passed into autumn, and Sam still could not force himself to leave the Cherokee and return to the white world. Only debts and work waited for him there. One afternoon, he stood with Oolooteka as small fires burned in the undergrowth of a grove of hickory trees. The nuts would be pounded into a sweet, rich milk. Sam caught sight of a scow cutting across the river from the garrison. Soon thereafter, Colonel Meigs walked toward them with a paper in hand.

"I have a report about the visit by the great Shawnee Chief Tecumseh at the Creek Council in Tuckabatchie," he said. "Tecumseh has called for the Creeks and Cherokee to join the British to fight against the Americans again."

Meigs eyed Sam. "Tell John Jolly that Colonel Meigs wants to know whether the chief will be friend or foe to the Americans."

Sam translated for his adoptive father.

Oolooteka stayed quiet for a few moments then told Sam to say, "Oolooteka is friend to all."

The day after, a messenger from the Bird Clan brought news of another council. It would be in five days' time, upriver at Savannah Ford. The Ridge would be giving a report of the meeting with Tecumseh and the Creeks.

Oolooteka told Sam, "Oolooteka needs to hear from the Ridge. Colonel Meigs twists too many words."

Together, they traveled along the north side of the river. Savannah Ford had the oldest council house in the valley. When Sam and Oolooteka rode into the small village, Sam saw the familiar gathering of liquor wagons off to one side. Chiefs—The Glass and Black Fox—were at the wagons. French Moran waved at him, but Sam only nodded, not wanting to leave Oolooteka.

"Sam, I have a message from your mother!" Moran yelled, motioning for him to come over.

Sam's heart lurched into his throat. He turned his pony and trotted quickly toward the wagons. "What is it?"

"She said to come home."

"Did she say why?"

"I believe the good woman simply wants to lay eyes on her wayward son." Moran held out a cup for Sam.

That didn't sound dire. Relieved to hear there was no emergency at home, like Paxton being on his deathbed, Sam waved off the offer of a taste of whatever spirits Moran was selling.

When the council began, a tall man with a long, pointed head stood first. He was the great sorcerer Tsali. His head had been plucked bald except for a sprig of hair that sprang from the crown. He wore a breechcloth only, despite the chill autumn air. The red paint under his eyes emphasized his high, prominent cheekbones and gave him a menacing look. No wolves attended the man, but Sam felt certain Tsali's blood could freeze a frog.

Tsali delivered his warning with great vigor and animation. "Forsake the white man's ways, and join Tecumseh's confederation with the British!"

He spoke for a long time, often casting his arms upward when invoking the Great Spirit. When Tsali stopped speaking, Sam expected more of a reaction. Instead, an uneasy silence spread among the audience. Perhaps the failure of Tsali's prediction had lessened the sorcerer's influence.

Next, the Ridge rose from his chair. Stout and confident, he declared, "War with the Americans will be our ruin. If Tecumseh comes to Cherokee territory with his talk of the warpath, he will be killed." For emphasis, the Ridge pointed his finger at the ground. "The earth did not shake and quiver as Tecumseh predicted. Tecumseh may stomp in his homeland, but the Cherokee do not feel it."

After another day of discussions, with many like Oolooteka siding with The Ridge, the Council voted to reject the call to join Tecumseh and the Creek.

As the others began to return to their homes, Oolooteka told Sam, "Oolooteka wants to see the land of his mother's ancestors."

Once mounted, they took a strenuous uphill trail that would have strained most horses. By midafternoon, they passed through the narrow gap where the Hiwassee's raging yellow rapids spilled through the mountains.

A few miles higher, Oolooteka pointed toward the mountains that sprawled in a northeasterly direction for miles. "That is the land of my mother's people."

They rounded a summit, and on the eastern slope lay a great, boundless body of placid water. Startled, Sam wondered if it was the Atlantic Ocean. But a few distant peaks on the far side poked through the smoky water. Like whispers, the topmost clouds slowly melted over the highest peaks, shifting and reshaping in a gentle caress that drifted lightly over the contours of the earth. Then the air stirred, and the sea vanished as though an invisible hand swept through the misty fog and laid bare a valley of infinite darkness. Tricked by his eyes, the base of Sam's spine puckered, and his feet shuffled in the stirrups as though to keep from falling. The spell broke when the pony jerked at the reins.

They rode on until they found a small spring to water the horses and set them to graze in the sparse undergrowth. The horse blankets kept them warm as the night air settled over the earth. During the long silence, an emptiness seemed to descend, and the air grew colder. The moon, now thinner and higher in the sky, was nearly lost among the clouds.

"The Cherokee have learned much from the white man, but our people do not need all that has been taught. The sun is our clock, and the moon is our calendar. The warming of the earth tells us when to plant seed. The tassel shows the corn will soon be ripe. When the leaves fall and the deer are rutting, we are warned the snow will descend and the wind will bite. Then we light the new fire, and before long, the grass is rising again."

As though hesitant to share the questions troubling his mind, Oolooteka spoke softly when he asked, "What will happen if the Creeks join with Tecumseh? How much will the Cherokee suffer when some of our young warriors take up their tomahawks against the Americans?"

"But the Ridge says the Cherokee will not join Tecumseh's confederation," Sam said.

Oolooteka stared into the fire. "Rattling Gourd listens to the Creeks."

Ah. Sam understood what Oolooteka feared. If Rattling Gourd took up the call to join with the Creeks, so would Oolooteka's son, Crying Bear.

"Why did Oolooteka put away the drum?" Sam asked in hopes of taking his adoptive father's mind off his worries about Crying Bear.

"Oolooteka didn't put away the drum. Oolooteka prefers to beat the drum of peace and happiness. The Cherokee warrior only wants to outdo his brothers in feats of arms. His is a restless spirit that desolates the earth. If war comes again, our people will lose our homeland. The Cherokee will all be forced into the darkening land of the dead."

Oolooteka's eyes glistened in the firelight, and tears streamed down his cheeks. Powerless, Sam was both afraid to offer trifling hopes or speak the inevitable truth. All he could give was his silent presence as a comfort to his adoptive father.

After a long silence, Oolooteka wiped his face and turned to Sam with a small grin.

"Kalunah talk more of your stories about the warriors, Achilles and Hector. And my sage friend, Chief Ulysses. How does he fare?"

Chapter Eight

When the Cold Moon began to wane, a message came from Tahlunteeskee. He told of a great earthquake near where the Cherokee had settled in their new land. The water in the Mississippi River had roiled up and flowed backward, and in large swaths, the land split in two, one side heaving up while the other side sank lower, leaving great gaps in the earth. Many of the villagers on Hiwassee Island were spooked by the news, but none worse than Oolooteka's wife. She begged Oolooteka to take her to see their son in Frogtown. Sam remembered Moran's message from his mother, to come home. That very night, Sam took his leave of Hiwassee Island.

"Kalunah will return when the grass is rising."

Guided by a large humpbacked moon, Sam walked toward Maryville. He'd not been home for over a year, not since the trouble with the sheriff. At midday, Sam found his mother in the loom house. Ma wore a pair of spectacles now and was a little more stooped in her posture. Polly and Eliza greeted him cheerfully, but Ma abruptly sent the girls away.

"How are you going to spend your life?" she asked him.

"Kalunah lives well with the Cherokee."

"Acquiring worldly riches is not the only measure in the Lord's eyes. And riches bought on credit invite trouble."

"But Kalunah is a friend to the Cherokee. As a linkster, he walks a straight path."

"Stop that Indian talk this minute." Her voice was sharp. She removed her glasses and glared at him. "You owe every trade house in Maryville. I can't imagine how much debt you've taken on."

"I'll settle those this winter."

"Sam, you're stealing from your own family. You have borrowed nearly thirty dollars from our store."

"My share will cover what I owe the store."

"Five dollars already went to pay the fine to the sheriff last year."

Sam hated to be reminded. "Surely, my share is worth more than that."

"You have an eighth share now. But even so, you must work off your debt or bring in payment, either coin or barter. I can't have you shirking your responsibilities when everyone else does their part to provide for the family."

"An eighth?" Sam asked.

Ma breathed in deeply and folded her hands in her lap. "Paxton has gone to the Lord."

Sam's voice broke when he asked, "When?"

"He caught a chill not two weeks ago."

Sam turned away. *Paxton… Oh, Paxton!* His brother had died, and Sam hadn't been around. A terrible barrenness filled his chest, taking him back to the moment on the summit when the fog cleared and all Sam had seen was blackness at his feet. Perhaps that had been the moment of Paxton's spirit passing over. Maybe Sam had felt his brother leaving this world. It brought him to tears—he'd abandoned Paxton by going to live among the Cherokee.

Ma kept talking, but Sam was lost in his grief and guilt and regret and didn't hear her for a few moments.

"After your father died, I paid every debt he left behind. We could have had a whole lot more of your fancy if I'd refused to honor his memory."

His mother's chest heaved and fell with a deep sigh. "Sam, I will not allow you to tarnish the family's name. This is a question of your character."

Sam finally met her eyes. Ma's strength and dignity were still there, but the years had taken their toll on her face. Dark circles had appeared under her eyes, and her lips turned down in heavy folds where a smile would have once been. Her stare never wavered, as strong and fierce as ever.

"Know this, my son: a dishonorable man is never welcome in my house. Do not darken my door again until you have settled your debts."

Sam walked away in a stupor. His mind searched for a place to go. The hunting cabins would be full that time of year. He couldn't return to Hiwassee Island and Oolooteka, not without gifts. The forcefulness of his mother's words made him question everything from the past. She'd always been his most ardent defender, the one from whom he could wheedle small favors and forgiveness. She'd never closed him off like that before, never taken the drastic step of barring the door in his face. No doubt, the Holy Apostles had wanted his mother to do so a long time before. They would be sure to keep Sam away until he settled his accounts.

He picked up the trail that led to Southwest Point. After a short distance, he started to see the world around him again, to hear the birds, to feel the cold when the sun fell behind a cloud, and to sense the wind on his face. About halfway through his journey, Sam came upon a clearing where a bear stood at a bee tree. He reached for his flint box then hesitated because suddenly, the bear became a symbol, an omen.

If he shot the animal, the fur might fetch a dollar. He could offer the meat and grease as a contribution to his debt to the family store. The thought of going back and groveling to James and John was intolerable. The Holy Apostles would take it as a sign Sam had submitted to their guardianship. He'd already given up on ever living at Baker Creek again.

The bear clawed at the beehive, sopping up honey with a paw, oblivious to both the attacking swarm of drones and Sam's presence. He would never reach his aspirations living the life of a trapper and hunter. *There is more to me, but where to find it?* Sam walked on and, in a couple of hours, stood behind Sheffy's counter, a measuring tape in hand.

After a month of earnings, Sam was able to purchase the necessary gifts for his return to Hiwassee Island. He wanted to bring Oolooteka something special and chose a leather belt. For himself, Sam bought a buckskin jacket with a beaver-fur collar. Sheffy made Sam pay steeply for the fancy items. As usual, Sam left still in debt to the store.

On a dull February morning, Sam paid fifty cents to ride a keelboat on its way to New Orleans. Fog hovered over the Tennessee River and hid the trees along the banks with only the tallest part of the canopy visible. The water flowed smoothly. The keening of birds and the occasional lone plaintive cry gave Sam a sense of passage beyond the distance traveled.

When he arrived on Hiwassee Island, Sam presented Oolooteka with the belt and gave out the other small tokens of friendship and gratitude. He heard no talk of joining the Creeks but sensed a nervous tension around Oolooteka. Sam wanted to ask about the visit with Crying Bear, but Oolooteka didn't say anything, and Sam didn't ask.

He knew he couldn't remain on the island forever. Over the next few weeks, his mood often turned blue. Even his favorite book couldn't offer much comfort:

> "The proud heart feels not terror nor turns to run,
> It is his own courage that kills him."

What courage do I have?

When he went to take his leave, he did not tell Oolooteka, "Kalunah will return." Instead, with his knapsack heavy on his shoulder and his rifle in hand, Sam said solemnly, "Kalunah must find his distinction in the white man's world."

Oolooteka put a hand at Sam's elbow, the Cherokee gesture of kinship. "The Great Spirit sees that Kalunah walks the straight path and talks the good talk. He will protect you on your journey. Oolooteka waits for when we meet again."

The parting brought on a terrible sense of loss, as though the easy confidence in his friendship with Oolooteka would never be the same. His absence would add to his adoptive father's growing burden. Tahlunteeskee had gone west, and Kalunah was leaving too.

Sam walked back to Sheffy's, and after another month working behind the counter, he'd saved ten dollars. He gave some of his earnings to the merchants in Maryville, offering small allotments to each, but reserved the largest sum, four dollars, for his mother. Ma accepted the money graciously but was unwavering in her resolve that Sam must earn his way back into the family fold. He didn't tell her he would never come home for good.

"Mr. Kennedy said he and Henry McCulloch are seeking a schoolmaster. I told him you would call on him about the position.

Do not disappoint me."

"Where?"

"North of here. Near the Little River. You would board with Mr. McCulloch's family. Six dollars a student. Between them, they have eleven sons."

The idea of teaching school captured Sam's imagination. Lately, as he worked his way through the eight volumes of Thucydides and was now reading *Caesar's Commentaries*, Sam had often wished for someone to converse with about what he read. Maybe working as a schoolmaster was a stepping stone to higher education.

Sam walked through Maryville and another five miles northeast before he reached the schoolhouse near a place called Cave Rolling Mill, where Kennedy ran a mill on the Little River. Mr. Kennedy had reddish-blond hair and a large chin that jutted from his skull. His dull-gray eyes were half hidden under heavy lids.

"Mrs. Houston tells me you read and write the best of all her boys."

"My mother speaks the truth. Sam has read more books than anyone in the whole family."

"I want my boys to learn to read and write and cipher to the single rule of three. Some of the local men, Henry McCulloch and Peter Brakebill, have tried their hand at teaching, but nothing seems to stick."

"Sir, they will learn from Sam to know their letters and know history and geography and how to calculate interest to guard against a swindler's loan."

"We paid the last schoolmaster six dollars a student. You'll need to talk to Henry McCulloch. He's got two boys."

Sam traveled a few miles to the south, where McCulloch kept a farm with a small cabin. McCulloch had three older daughters and two younger sons.

"You can sleep here and take your meals with the family," McCulloch told Sam as though the job were already his for the taking.

"Why'd the last schoolmaster leave?" Sam asked, now a little suspicious at the man's eagerness.

"Well, that second son of Kennedy gave him a good licking when the schoolmaster called him stupid and lazy."

Sam went to meet with Mr. Kennedy again. "Sam will become the schoolmaster, but he needs eight dollars a student."

Kennedy snorted. "That's two dollars more!"

"Sam can take a third in corn at thirty-three cents a bushel and a third in calico cloth. He needs the coin before the session starts."

The money would pay off his remaining debts, the corn he could barter with for other necessities, and the cloth he could use to have shirts made, since his mother wouldn't be providing for him.

Kennedy wavered, "Well, I don't know…"

"Sam has a dictionary, an atlas, and many other books he will use for the reading lessons."

"I've already paid plenty for primers and slate boards. Another two dollars is a steep price."

"If primers and slate boards were good enough, you wouldn't need Sam Houston for a schoolmaster."

Kennedy hesitated for a moment. "Your mother said you spoke like an Indian. You bargain like one too."

"Sam speaks like Julius Caesar and only asks for his just tribute."

Kennedy then showed Sam where some primers and other materials had been left by the former schoolmasters. Sam collected twenty-four dollars and three cents from Kennedy. He went straight to Baker Creek and handed to his mother what he still owed to the family store. The Holy Apostles were standing at her side.

John snickered loudly. "Mr. Kennedy must be desperate to hire you with your Indian degree."

James took the coin from Ma's hand. "You still owe six dollars to the store."

Sam borrowed a small cart to carry the crate of books from the family's barn up to the schoolhouse. The one-room cabin was situated in a small clearing surrounded by a heavy wood, with no prospect of the mountains. On the first day of classes, the pale morning light came on slowly while Sam stood listening to the early chatter of birds. He spied an owl high in a tree, framed against the coming light. The bird opened its wings, seemed about to fly, but then settled again on the tree. Another owl called from a distance, and the owl in the tree answered before it spread its wings and rose upward with a flap. The owl seemed to float in the air then silently disappeared into the woods.

Sam propped open the schoolhouse door, two inches thick and hung with leather gun hitches. Inside was a crude fireplace and a small wooden desk near a granny hole in the corner. The desk was like the one his mother had kept in Virginia. Sam didn't remember learning to read and had no memory of not understanding the alphabet, but his mother's hand on his had taught him to write. He brushed those memories aside before striding toward the narrow windows on the south wall. The long shutters were fastened with a hinge along the bottom edge and could be turned into makeshift desks. Sam lowered the first one. With wooden legs as props, the shutter stood well for the taller students. Sam propped open the second tall window and the lower one on the west side for the smaller boys. Three hand-hewn puncheon benches provided the seating.

McCulloch's two boys, ten and twelve years old, arrived first. Sam stood just inside the doorway, a hickory switch in hand. The boys took seats in the front.

The four youngest Kennedy boys trickled in. Sam flicked the switch against each one's leg as he passed by. They scurried over and took seats on the middle bench. When the first of the older Kennedy boys came through, Sam grabbed him by his collar, announcing, "This is your first lesson today!"

Against the boy's backside, Sam offered a few quick, decisive strikes with the switch. The boy hurried to the back bench. The next three Kennedys were handled as easily.

The troublemaking ringleader was the last to arrive. Only a few inches shorter than Sam, this Kennedy boy had the same light-red hair and prominent jaw as the father. When Sam grabbed him, the boy leapt and tried to free himself, kicking his heels up and hopping around. Sam held his grip and set the hickory switch to whistling the song of discipline on the younger boy's backside.

The other kids laughed and howled, the Kennedy brothers rooting for their brother and the McCullochs cheering for Sam. The ringleader finally submitted and took the last seat on the back bench.

Then Sam began testing each boy's knowledge. He started with the oldest Kennedy, asking him to recite the alphabet and do simple sums. Sam gave no indication of the students' abilities but simply rearranged the seating according to ability. The older McCulloch boy was the best at math. Sam put him at the front of the advanced group. When he assigned the ringleader Kennedy boy to the lowest grade level, the troublemaker refused to move, declaring, "I can spell as good as anyone."

"I am running this class. You'll sit where I think you belong," Sam said.

The ringleader jumped up. "My father will have you horsewhipped."

"The only one who'll be whipped is you!" In an instant, Sam was lashing the switch against the boy's legs in quick measure.

The Kennedy boy hopped and skipped and yelped like a dog but refused to give in.

"Let me know when you've had enough of this lesson." Sam grabbed a fistful of the ringleader's hair and dragged him to the front bench and forced him to sit.

The ringleader's face was red and sweaty, with his jaw thrust forward in unmistakable resentment, but he remained where Sam had put him. For a solid minute, Sam stared down at the ringleader, waiting for the boy's anger to burn itself out. His eyes never left the boy, and the ringleader squirmed on the bench, shifting his feet anxiously with his arms hugging his chest until, like a bubble burst, the boy's jaw relaxed, his arms fell to his sides, and he whined, "Stop! Please stop staring at me, and I'll do what you say."

Sam turned his attention to the class, and without any reference to the unpleasantness, he patiently set the advanced boys at the window desks, assigning each a lesson from the primer. The youngest boys in the lower group were given slate boards to practice their penmanship. Then Sam had the ringleader and his older brother come to the schoolmaster's desk near the granny hole. He placed the atlas between them and opened the book to a map of the Mediterranean Sea.

"This is the place of a great battle." He pointed at Tunisia and began the story of the Battle of Zama on the shores of Africa.

The boys stared at the map, their eyes wide with curiosity.

Later, Sam read aloud from a book of poems by Robert Burns, spelling out the words on the slate boards so the students could take turns copying what he'd written. As the days passed, Sam began to use the oldest McCulloch boy to help him teach the arithmetic lessons. He would call the boy to the front of the room and give him a problem to solve.

"Say you have five bushels of corn and the store clerk offers you fifty cents a bushel. How much money should you receive?"

"Two dollars and fifty cents."

"Mark that out for everyone to see."

Using the slate board, the McCulloch boy scribbled the equation with chalk.

"Son, you have a good command of ciphering, but your penmanship needs some attention," Sam said with a chuckle.

The other boys laughed, but it wasn't with derision, rather admiration and respect.

At the end of each day, Sam would recite lines from *The Iliad*. He would look out at the eager faces, their eyes attentive, their minds open and their voices quiet, wholly lost in the magical spell cast by the story of Achilles, Hector, Ajax, and Ulysses. The power of his voice and the command he held over the once unruly Kennedy boys filled Sam with a pride he'd never known before.

Soon, word got around, and Sam had over twenty students in the classroom. The oldest—a man twice Sam's age—had never learned his letters or numbers. From then on, Sam used a sourwood switch as an instrument of instruction rather than a threat of discipline. His long chestnut hair he kept tied at the nape of his neck and hanging in a queue down his back. Sam wore his collar open, and the thick auburn hair on his chest appeared like a buffalo mop. He could speak for hours, enthralling the boys with tales of the famous battles of the ancient world.

At the noon hour, Sam would take the class down by the rivulet that poured cool spring water, nearly hidden in the tall grass. He shared from the basket Mrs. McCulloch sent with her sons, usually filled with biscuits and butter and a few bites of cold meat. After eating, the boys washed in the small stream and either retired under the shade of a tree or romped around for an hour or so.

In early summer, a bramble of dewberries ripened nearby. Before class, Sam let the boys pick the small berries off vines thick with thorns. Black juice stained their hands, and their fingers were pricked with red dots where thorns had broken through skin. In the afternoons, he gave a history lesson, perhaps on the Revolutionary War or Leonidas leading the Spartans to their tragic fall against the

Persians. With every new volume he read, Sam brought back another piece of history to his students. The boys soon began to fight over who would hold the atlas so that Sam could point out where the battles took place.

In the fall, Sam taught the boys to make ball sticks out of hickory wood and play the Cherokee ball game, using heavy green walnuts for a ball. Instead of scoring goals, the object became how to avoid the mighty sting from those hard cannonball-sized missiles.

After the second school session ended, Sam had enough to pay off his remaining debts in Maryville. Emboldened by the sense of achievement, he was determined to study Latin and Greek, because Sam was obviously meant to be a scholar.

Porter Academy had a new schoolmaster, Isaac Anderson. Sam used his last few dollars to enroll and stayed on at the McCulloch farm. Mr. Anderson eagerly set out a course of study for Sam to follow. The plan included Euclid, and for a few weeks, he carried a book of geometry equations with him, but not once did he lift the book cover. The classes were stifling affairs, for Mr. Anderson lectured with all the enthusiasm of an afternoon nap. Before long, Sam was either late or didn't appear at all. When it came time to pay for another session, Sam admitted he couldn't tolerate algebra or geometry.

"I won't say I'm surprised," Mr. Anderson said with a grin. "But I will miss those pretty dishes you serve as excuses for missing class and not doing your lessons."

As winter came on, Sam was debt free, but he needed something to live on. He used the handcart to bring his crate of books back to the family barn.

"You're welcome to move home." Ma's offer sounded both hopeful and despondent.

"Thank you, Ma. But Sam must make his own way in the world."

Chapter Nine

"Sam!" Robert McEwen, Sam's second cousin, stood in the doorway to the back storeroom at Sheffy's, where Sam was cleaning out a barrel of pickles gone rancid.

Sam stretched the kinks from his back. Earlier that morning, he'd woken in the middle of a nightmare that left him in a mood as sour as the pickles. In the dream, he was on the journey to Tennessee, frustrated because he'd lost the path. Paxton and Polly were with him, but he couldn't find where Ma had gone. He searched helplessly for the trail and Ma, finding himself on the same mountain he'd sat on at fifteen. In the dream, the rocks beneath his feet began to crumble, and Sam tumbled down and over a cliff. Before he hit the ground, he woke with a jolt—a troubling omen for the start of his twentieth birthday.

"The Seventh is coming," Robert said.

The Americans were at war with the British again, exactly as the Shawnee Chief Tecumseh had predicted. The week before, the Tennessee Militia had been in town, recruiting men to fight against the Creeks who had taken up the cause with Tecumseh. Sam didn't know whether the Cherokee held fast to their pledge of neutrality. Surely, Oolooteka would not fight, but others like Rattling Gourd might have gone to war with the Creek.

Halfway out of the store, Robert called, "C'mon, Willoughby's waiting."

Sam didn't share his cousin's excitement. His years with the Cherokee had divided his loyalties. Most recently, he'd been isolated in the schoolhouse, and ever since leaving Porter Academy, Sam wasn't quite sure where he fit in. He stepped out into a blinding light. A brisk zephyr carrying the scent of spring whipped around Sam. He pulled his hat down. Robert and young Willoughby Williams were out in the lane, eagerly awaiting the parade of soldiers. Sam didn't hurry to join them, not yet.

Robert would soon be entering Washington College in east Tennessee, taking the path Sam had failed to follow. He didn't want to attend a strict Presbyterian school, but his cousin's impending departure made Sam increasingly dissatisfied with his own life, feeling that he'd somehow failed his younger self.

The drumbeat announced the 7th Infantry. A soldier bearing the standard paraded slowly down the lane. A fifer and two drummers followed next. The music swirled around a double column of soldiers, three deep, marching in fancy uniforms—white woolen pantaloons, blue waistcoats with stiff red collars and cuffs, and tall black boots. The Tennessee Militia wore drab dun-colored fringed frock coats.

The recruiting party stopped across the lane. Robert and Willoughby went to join the other spectators. Sam stayed back, brooding. At sixteen, he'd escaped his brothers' guardianship, but he couldn't say that he'd done anything worthwhile with his liberty. Trapped in a job he despised, wearing the previous year's clothes, and unable to afford a horse, he couldn't see how to escape his bleak and dismal existence. He let out a deep, forlorn sigh.

The soldiers broke form. The drummer removed his instrument and set it on the ground. Sam didn't see a cask of cider or rum like the Tennessee Militia had offered. A tall lieutenant stepped forward and held a silver coin high above his head. "There's a dollar to every recruit who enlists today."

The silver caught the light, gleaming for a moment. Sam crossed the lane and went to stand with Robert and Willoughby just as the lieutenant dramatically set the coin on the drum.

"C'mon, boys. Thicken your blood by defending your country. Remember that when England once ruled our land, a lowly British officer, fresh off the frigate from London, lorded over and commanded the father of our country. Yes, George Washington, a seasoned and experienced commander, hardened by the French and

Indian War, could be pressed into service by any dunce of an ensign."

Some in the crowd laughed. Others booed.

"We fight because of this unfairness and the loss of the freedom and liberty that we are accustomed to now. American sailors are being impressed into British service. Our ports are blockaded, tariffs levied against our goods. Our fathers and grandfathers died for our country. Will we let their deaths be in vain?"

The lieutenant turned and seemed to address Sam directly. Unexpectedly, the possibilities of life as a soldier sprang to mind. The infantry would give Sam a splendid uniform. He'd be fed and housed and paid. He didn't need a horse in the infantry. Without a second thought, Sam stepped through the crowd and plucked the silver dollar off the drum.

Immediately, a sergeant hustled him toward a makeshift table. They took his name, but when they learned he wasn't twenty-one yet, they said he needed his mother's permission to enlist. Sam held the slip of paper when he returned to Robert's side.

"If you wanted to join the fight, why didn't you enlist with the militia?" Robert asked. "They don't care how old you are. With your family's name, you'd muster in as an officer. My cousin James is a captain with Colonel Benton. He's your age and on his way to New Orleans with General Jackson."

Sam felt a tinge of regret—this was another example of what the years he'd spent with the Cherokee had cost him in terms of knowledge and experience in the white world.

Willoughby piped up. "You can say your mother wouldn't grant permission and then sign up with the militia."

"I can't afford to join the militia," Sam said bleakly. "The only thing they give you is a musket."

He'd made his choice, taken a direction, and started on a path, and he wouldn't turn back. After taking leave from Mr. Sheffy, Sam walked home to Baker Creek.

When he gave the paper to his mother, she stared at him. "Why haven't they given you an officer's commission? Your brother Robert is a captain in Virginia. Surely, once they know who your father was, you'd receive a commission."

"Sam won't ride on his father's coattails. He will make a name for himself."

"The enlistment is five years." Ma looked at Sam with genuine concern.

James sat at the desk. "He'll not last three days, whether in the ranks or as an officer. The first time Sam is ordered to do something he doesn't like or that disturbs his tender sensibilities, he'll run away like he always does."

"I'll write to my brother. You'll be an officer in the Virginia Militia. That's where you belong instead of this." Ma waved the paper.

John sneered at Sam. "He'd disgrace any appointment they'd give him, Ma. Let him go to it. He'll be in good stead with the raw recruits. The educated fool with his Indian degree. At last, Sam will be first among his peers, most of whom are dumb as chickens."

Full of anger, indignation, and the resentment of wounded pride, Sam yelled, "And what have your craven souls to say about the ranks? You don't respect me now, but you will hear of me when I rise above you all."

Reluctantly, Ma signed the waiver. As she gave him the paper, she said, "Sam, a coward can never return to my home. I would rather bury all my sons as heroes than have one son turn his back and run."

Midafternoon on the twenty-fourth of March, Sam sighted the tents along a broad flattop hill northeast of Nashville. Directed to Captain McClellan's tent, Sam mustered in. After measuring his height and noting his birthplace, a secretary marked his name and particulars in a large entry book. Captain McClellan's mouth and chin caved inward, but he observed Sam with a keen, businesslike eye.

"Samuel—" McClellan began.

"I go by Sam, sir."

McClellan turned to a sergeant and said, "Take Private Sam Houston to Company G."

The next day, Sam stood with the other recruits as a lieutenant read out the *Articles of War* before a magistrate. He received a musket with a bayonet and learned to load, fire, and thrust in the disciplined movements of a military formation. Within a week, Sam was leading the drill for the thirty-eight recruits.

Spring had asserted herself with dewdrops on the tender grass, green buds on the tips of trees, and the wild hyacinth blooming in the meadows. The fresh scent of new life on the wind made this a magnificent time. Sam took to the soldier's life, learning to set up camp—digging trenches for protection and latrines, raising tents, and organizing in squads for guard duty. About a month later, when the bonfires of azaleas—fuchsia, violet, flaming orange—bloomed in the hills, Captain McClellan called Sam to report to headquarters.

"Today, Sam Houston, you have been promoted."

With stripes added to the shoulders of his waistcoat, Sam was a sergeant. The captain gave him a copy of the *Articles of War.* "You will need this to enforce the rules and regulations."

Looking down, Captain McClellan dismissed Sam with one last command. "You're assigned to the quartermaster's unit. Report to Lieutenant Whitehead."

Thrust into the belly of the infantry, his first job was to help with provisioning the regiment for their two-hundred-fifty-mile march to the Alabama territory. Sam accompanied Lieutenant Whitehead to nearby Knoxville. With only a government IOU for payment, they bartered, haggled, begged, and scavenged for blankets, food, feed, and ammunition from the local merchants. A company of six hundred soldiers and two hundred horses required bushels of grain, tons of tack, either beef or venison, cured pork, and many hundredweights of miscellaneous goods.

What seemed most remarkable in those days came from the recognition Sam received. Every sign of initiative brought more responsibility and prestige. As the days grew longer, he spent the evenings with the last rays of sunlight illuminating the pages of the *Articles of War,* most of which had been written by General Washington himself. Sam's fast progression satisfied his restless and ambitious spirit.

The march to Fort Hampton began in mid-August. Sam had command of a platoon of fifty-eight men and twelve wagon teams when the regiment left camp. Their journey followed the western shore of the Tennessee River. When they neared the Hiwassee Garrison, where they would procure more supplies, Sam felt a strong desire to ask for a scow to cross the river so he could visit his adoptive father. But his responsibilities outweighed the sentiment.

The regiment camped along the banks of the river, just opposite from where Sam had had his bark lean-to on Hiwassee Island. Amidst the hum of activity, Sam found a moment to walk to the river's edge. In the afternoon light, the dragonflies were thick around him. He watched as a pair mated on a leaf of milkweed, floating in and out of a shaft of fading sunlight, the insects shiny blue-black in one instant, dull and colorless the next. He picked out the roof of Oolooteka's house among the trees. A painful nostalgia overtook him. The people who had welcomed Sam as family were so close yet a world away.

The next morning, an ensign with a propensity for whiskey had fallen asleep at his post. A quick court-martial ensued, resulting in the officer being cashiered—stripped of his commission, his epaulets ripped from his uniform, and sent down as a private. McClellan divided the ensign's platoon among the others, giving Sam command of another twenty-four soldiers.

The officers were quickly taking notice of Sam's mastery of the horse teams. He could stage a difficult passage and take the reins in a jam. In late August, the regiment reached Fort Hampton, a blockade positioned on a hill above the Elk River, just north of where it flowed into the Tennessee. When they marched into the palisade, Sam had command of a platoon of one hundred ninety-six men and thirty-three wagons.

Very quickly, guarding the fort became routine, reminding Sam too much of clerking. That raised the old feelings of restlessness, the irresistible need to get away. Finally, the monotony broke when a unit of artillery arrived. Captain Deaderick came with orders to remove the howitzer and take it to the Tennessee Militia. He didn't come empty-handed, for he brought news of a massacre at Fort Mims.

Three hundred miles south, on the Tenasa River, close to Spanish territory, Fort Mims had suffered a brutal attack by a group of Creek warriors who'd joined with Tecumseh's federation. They carried clubs painted red and called themselves the Red Sticks. In hushed voices, some of the soldiers in Deaderick's unit claimed a drunken Major Beasley had disregarded warnings about a gathering force. When a thousand warriors under Red Eagle arrived eager for bloodshed, the east gate stood unprotected and ajar. In the end, four hundred Americans died savagely. The massacre caused the war to become about more than simply defending America's ports against the British. Talk of General Jackson recruiting for the fight against the Red Sticks swept through the fort. Most everyone hoped the 7th Infantry would join with the Tennessee Militia in the fight with the Red Sticks.

Deaderick also brought a packet of orders and correspondence for Captain McClellan. To his great surprise, Sam received another promotion. He would join the 39th as an ensign. In four months' time, Sam had achieved the officer's commission Ma had hoped for, but he'd done it on merit alone, with no help from his family or friends. He still felt the scorn from the Holy Apostles and the ridicule from his cousins at Houston Station, for they'd all cut him off. But Sam was taking pride and pleasure in proving how little his family and friends knew his true character.

His adoptive father, Oolooteka, would have understood. Sam couldn't labor as an indentured servant forever, always in debt and beholden to Mr. Sheffy. For the Cherokee, that was the coward's path. It would have led to Sam's ruin.

In a few days' time, Sam and several others left Fort Hampton for the return trip to Knoxville. When he reported to duty, Colonel Williams didn't even give Sam a glance. Without looking up, he simply stated, "Captain McClellan writes you're a good quartermaster."

The colonel never met Sam's eye, which made Sam feel pigeonholed and uneasy. What Captain McClellan might have lacked in inspiration, he made up for by taking the time to judge a man by his accomplishments and his abilities. Colonel Williams behaved like a store clerk, treating a man as a stock item to be positioned on a shelf.

Sam was assigned to Lt. Colonel Benton's unit. A man the size of a bear, Thomas Hart Benton was tall, broad, and muscular, with a ferocious growl when he gave orders. The three other junior officers welcomed Sam into the unit with a cold, indifferent manner, reminding him of how his brothers James and John treated him. Days passed before Sam heard the shocking news that General Jackson had been wounded in a duel. He knew about dueling, but he'd never actually known anyone who'd been in one. The exact reason for the duel differed, depending upon who told the story. Then Sam began to notice his fellow officers' attitude toward Lt. Colonel Benton, as though Benton had the pox. From his experience with the 7th Infantry, Captain McClellan always had an officer as an aide by his side. But Sam's peers kept their distance, only approaching Benton if required. When he questioned an ensign about it, the man answered, "Who wants to stand near the most hated man in Tennessee?"

"Benton? Why is he the most hated man?"

"Don't you know? He's the one who shot General Jackson."

Shocked, Sam wanted to know more, but he wasn't sure whose version to trust. Like Oolooteka said, "A man doesn't need to listen to bad talks."

A few days later, Sam went with Benton on a recruiting party to Jonesborough, a half-day's ride east. The party was small, only a fifer and drummer and Sam carrying the standard. To his surprise, Lt. Colonel Benton gave a rousing and vigorous speech in front of the Chester Inn. A dozen men enlisted without the enticement of a silver dollar.

"We'll see how many muster in," Benton told Sam as they started on the return trip, riding side-by-side.

The air was cool and dry and still. The tree canopy above the trail held the last remnants of the blood and gold of autumn, but the path was mostly littered with crisp, dun-colored leaves crunching under the horses' hooves.

"I'm a dead man. You know that, don't you?" Benton cocked his head and lifted an eyebrow.

"You look mighty alive to me."

Benton laughed. "I don't know what you've heard, but I tried to avoid him, you know. The General and Colonel Coffee, they came after us after they learned Jesse and I were in Nashville. When I refused to fight him, Jackson put his horsewhip to me."

Sam's stomach jumped to his throat, but he waited to hear more, sensing that Benton needed to unburden his conscience. They rode a little farther, and Benton sounded almost wistful when he said, "The General was like a father to me, but his treatment of Jesse was dishonorable."

"How so?"

"They played a dirty trick on my brother when Jesse challenged Carroll to a duel. The General knows that Carroll is a poor marksman. He acted as Carroll's second, and Jesse was shot in the ass. He was the laughingstock of Nashville for weeks." Benton turned and glared at Sam as though reliving the insult. "I couldn't let that stand. I called the general out for his misdeeds. He'd have done the same."

A goose honked. Sam glanced up at a flock of snow geese in the sky, thinking of the words Black Fox had spoken at Ustinali: "Of all the wars, none is so dreadful as those between brothers."

"I hear General Jackson remains at the Hermitage, recuperating." No animosity remained in Benton's voice. "The Tennessee Militia is signing up recruits for two-month terms. If the general isn't well enough to mount a horse, he'll lose his soldiers before he can bring the fight to the Red Sticks."

Benton pushed a low-hanging branch away from his head. "I'll be leaving for Missouri soon. No sense staying in Tennessee. Jackson is a powerful man, and I still admire him above all others. I wish it hadn't happened. I didn't want to fight him, not after all we went through. When General Wilkinson abandoned us in Natchez, half the men were frail with dysentery…"

Sam recognized the name Wilkinson. He'd heard vague references to a failed campaign in the Louisiana Territory, so he listened carefully to the firsthand account.

"Jackson gave up his horse so the weakest could ride while he walked with his men. That's when they started calling him Old Hickory. The general can take anything! A ball to his shoulder, and Old Hickory will come back fighting harder than ever. I've seen it. That's why he won't let me anywhere near the fight with the Red Sticks."

Sam wondered if General Jackson would really bar Benton from the battlefield over a personal dispute. Sam's brother John was petty and vengeful. *Is the general the same? If the stories about his honor and loyalty are even half true, how can he treat Benton this poorly?*

"Now, Sam, you're a young man with ambitions. Ask for another promotion."

"How?"

"Didn't you write for this commission?"

Sam shook his head.

"Well then, your friends did it for you. Even more reason to seek a promotion."

Sam considered who might have done it—surely, neither of the Holy Apostles. Perhaps Ma had written to her brother.

Benton smiled at Sam. "You'll do well. I can see that already. I'll sing your praises. I still have friends in Washington."

Another flock of birds—ducks that time—flew overhead in a noisy V. Sam watched as the lead bird dropped back and the next duck smoothly slipped into place, a flawless transition that would have made a drillmaster proud.

Chapter Ten

Sure enough, Lt. Colonel Benton remained behind when the 39th Infantry began the two-hundred-mile trek to Jackson's camp deep in the heart of Red Sticks territory. Assigned to the quartermaster unit again, Sam had charge of the baggage train of supplies and ammunition this time. Although cold, their march along the Tennessee River was steady. Before reaching the Hiwassee Garrison, they turned westward, and the trail narrowed, but the hills were softer, with fewer steep grades.

In early February, the 39th paraded into Fort Strother. Sam hoped to see, maybe even meet, the great man. But the conditions inside the fort shocked him. The soldiers did not have enough tents, and the enclosures for livestock stood bare. The men were lean and glum and their horses underfed. In quick order, Sam learned that a court-martial had been held only a few days earlier. The officer was acquitted, but the threat of mutiny still hung ripe among the lower ranks. The loudest grumbling came from the 3rd Regiment of Tennessee Volunteers. Those men had enlisted on the promise they'd soon be home after a quick fight. Many came without proper clothing, and now, away from their farms, their families were left unprepared for winter.

Seeing the dire situation of the militia and thinking of the Cherokees' hospitality when others were in need, Sam suggested the 39th share their provisions with the starving men.

"We'll need the supplies for the march to New Orleans," the quartermaster answered abruptly.

"General Jackson has asked for the 39th to stay. We could afford half rations for a few days," Sam argued.

"Learn this lesson well, Ensign. Never, ever give up what's yours unless ordered to do so."

But the constant struggle for food, clothing, blankets, and ammunition made Sam anxious until, a few days later, the long-awaited battalion under Major Clark arrived with the provisions. Some of the more desperate men clambered around the wagons. Sam stepped in to protect the supplies and stayed on as a guard while the quartermasters from the different units began their haggling. Hours passed before he learned Major Clark had brought orders—the 39th would stay with Jackson's army to fight the Red Sticks.

Lt. Colonel Benton had not forgotten his promise, for the packet of mail also brought news of Sam's promotion to third lieutenant. And best of all, Sam was attached to Major Montgomery's company. Colonel Williams had remained indifferent toward Sam, who'd feared that, without Benton's support, the colonel would post Sam with the wagons in the rear guard. Major Montgomery's company had the best soldiers and would likely be at the front when the fighting started. At last, Sam would have a chance to prove his mettle in battle.

As their new commanding officer, General Jackson addressed the 39th. Tall and thin, he had a spike of bristly graying hair on his head. The striking blue eyes were set deep in a gaunt, angular face. Clearly, the general had suffered the same deprivations as his men. His voice reached out to Sam, firm and strong.

"From our excursions with the Red Sticks at Emuckfaw and Enotachopco, I have discovered the enemy are more vigilant than usual. They are well armed and supplied with powder of the best kind, and they are determined to avoid anything like a close engagement with us.

"There will be an opportunity offered you of manifesting your zeal to your country and avenging the cruelties committed upon our defenseless fellow citizens. In the hour of battle, you must be cool and collected. When your officer orders you to fire, you must execute the command with deliberateness and aim. Let every shot tell."

Jackson paused, his spine straightening.

"Any officer or soldier who flies before the enemy without being compelled to do so by superior force and actual necessity shall suffer death."

From that moment forward, Jackson's army presented a brave new world for Sam—life and death with no time for reflection or reading. Spies came and went, orders were given out in formal readings, and speculation ran rampant about the coming fight with the Red Sticks. Not long afterward, a band of two hundred mounted Cherokee arrived. The Ridge and Rising Fawn were leading the warriors, but Sam had no time to remake any of his Cherokee acquaintances. The Tennessee Militia was in turmoil again. Word spread quickly that a young volunteer in the 3rd Regiment had refused an order to return to his post. The general flew into a rage, cursing and demanding the young boy be shot. A court-martial was called, and within a day, the judge declared Private John Wood guilty.

Colonel Williams pleaded for leniency. In answer, Jackson ordered the 39th to perform the execution. Sam volunteered for guard duty. A tent served as a makeshift jail. Wood told his story to Sam in the quiet hours after midnight.

"I was hired as a substitute. They said it would only be for a short time. My parents need me. No man should have to answer to another after he's served his time."

Sam felt sorry for the hapless youth, and he hoped General Jackson would spare Wood from the firing squad. After the bugle sounded reveille, a letter for Private Wood arrived.

The prisoner handed the letter to Sam. "I can't read that good." Then he hung his head over hands clasped tightly together.

Sam cleared his throat and unfolded the pages. The letter was in Andrew Jackson's own hand.

"The offenses of which you have been found guilty are such as cannot be permitted to pass unpunished in an army but at the hazard of its ruin."

As though in agreement, young Wood nodded his head.

Sam read on, "An army cannot exist where order and subordination are wholly disregarded. The disobedience of orders and the contempt of officers speedily lead to a state of disorganization and ruin and mutiny. This is an important crisis in which, if we all act as becomes us, everything is to be hoped for toward the accomplishment of the objects of our government. If otherwise, everything is to be feared. How it becomes us to act, we all know, and what our punishment shall be if we act otherwise, must be known also."

Jackson's words spoke directly to Sam. No leniency would be provided for Private Wood. Sam did not witness the execution, but he heard the report of the rifle when it occurred. Odd as it seemed, the death of Private John Wood was like the bright day that sometimes follows a deadly storm. The question of leniency was put to rest, and if any grumbling occurred among the men, it never found Sam's ears.

Less than two days later, Jackson ordered the 39th to establish a staging camp downriver. They took flatboats on the Coosa River, putting in at the mouth of Cedar Creek. Sam worked with his platoon to dig trenches and build berms as fortifications against a surprise attack by the Red Sticks. Once the camp was secure, all the forces under Jackson's command would come together.

Colonel Coffee's cavalry arrived first. With him were the mounted Cherokee, numbering five hundred warriors. The white feathers and white-tailed deer cockades on the Cherokees' hats distinguished them from the Red Sticks. Sam walked among the Cherokee and saw his friend, Little Otter.

Sam gripped Little Otter's forearm. "Why did you come back?"

"I brought a message from Tahlunteeskee to Hiwassee Island. Then I heard the call to join the warriors against the Red Sticks."

"How is Oolooteka?"

"Oolooteka stays away from the fight, but his son is here."

"Crying Bear is with the Red Sticks?"

"He is Running Bear now because he ran from Rattling Gourd to join with The Ridge."

Sam felt for Oolooteka, but at least his son was with the Ridge. A part of him longed to be with the Cherokee, and Sam couldn't resist asking, "Does Little Otter know the girl who spoke only English?"

"Virginia Patsy?"

Sam nodded, asking shyly, "How is she?"

"She's in Chatouga, married to a nephew of the Glass."

Sam didn't have time to ponder the news because the *rat-tat-tat* of drums announced the 2nd Regiment of Mounted Gunmen entering camp. They brought a wagon train of food and ammunition and

Sam's cousin Robert McEwen. Robert was a third lieutenant too, commissioned when he enlisted in Doherty's regiment.

Sam slapped his cousin on the back. "I thought you were at Washington College."

Robert laughed. "I couldn't let you take all the glory."

A powerful sense of belonging came over Sam. With his Cherokee brothers on one side and his Houston cousin on the other, he was exactly where he was meant to be. Flush with that indelible sense of destiny, Sam accompanied Major Montgomery to General Jackson's headquarters.

"Major, I want you to lead the front line," the general said.

Then something extraordinary happened. General Jackson turned his attention to Sam. The deep-set eyes gave off a warmth and friendliness that transformed the general's fierce countenance into the face of a gracious and cordial host, as though he were welcoming Sam into his home. The general asked Sam about his family, and Sam said his father had fought with Morgan's Riflemen.

"Ah, the son of a revolutionary hero," Jackson said with a smile. "And you are following the same path, defending your country. You have aspirations, I can see that."

The general's words of encouragement filled Sam with something akin to his love for Oolooteka, but the feeling held something more—loyalty beyond question. If asked, Sam would gladly follow Andrew Jackson into the pits of hell.

When the faint glow of predawn appeared behind the high hills in the east, the main body of Jackson's army began the march to Tohopeka. The drums of the 39th kept a vigorous pace, and soon, the bayonets glittered in the rising sun. Dew in the meadows sparkled while frost lingered in the shallow dips and hollows of the woodlands. The night before, Sam couldn't rest, wishing there'd been a dance to ready his body and his mind for the coming battle. He wondered if the Red Sticks had their own eagle-tail dance and if they knew the army was coming.

Filled with excitement and anticipation, Sam moved in a state of bliss, fueled by an energy that burned like coals smoldering in a hearth. His feet were on the ground, but his spirit was soaring in the skies like an eagle. Sam fantasized he was with Scipio Africanus, crossing the desert in Tunisia. When they trampled through abandoned fields, Sam pretended he was with Caesar in Gaul, and when passing through a wet glade, he thought of Washington on the shores of the Delaware. After the golden hour of daybreak vanished, remnants of the village of Emuckfaw appeared—huts burnt to the ground and fields set afire two months earlier, handiwork of the Tennessee Militia.

Tree stumps studded the landscape near the enemy's camp. In the near distance, small puffs of smoke rose over a large spit of land. The women and girls would be preparing the morning meal. The Red Sticks had chosen well the place to make their last stand. A tight bend in the Tallapoosa created a peninsula. A fortress of breastworks made of thick pine timbers zigzagged up from the western banks and crossed over the narrow neck of land stretching out into the water. The Red Sticks could easily defend themselves from a frontal attack. Before the march began, Coffee's cavalry and the mounted Cherokee and friendly Creek warriors had split off from the main army to cross downstream. They would guard the southern shore of the horseshoe bend, prepared to kill or capture any Red Sticks trying to escape.

Jackson's army hustled into position. Two cannons, a four-pounder and a six-pounder, were wheeled atop a small hill on the western flank. Montgomery's company formed the advance guard east of the cannon. From eighty yards away, Sam judged the rampart about five feet high. Then his eyes picked out the muzzles poking out from portholes fashioned between the logs.

The cannon boomed, and the first ball hit the barricade but bounced off, barely making a dent. A second ball bored into a log and stayed there. Smoke drifted lazily in the air then settled over the line of men, bringing a musty, acrid odor and the promise of action. The next cannon ball flew over the ramparts, followed by a terrifying scream from behind the barricade.

"Steady your nerves, men," Montgomery called. "It won't be long now."

Time passed under the strain of a tedious tension as dozens of cannonballs failed to make even the slightest damage to the fortifications. Low-lying clouds gathered in the sky, shielding the sun almost directly overhead. Montgomery kept his keen dark eyes leveled at the barricade, and Sam tried to model outward patience, but his body was tight on a tether, and despite the cool wind, his ears burned, and his cheeks were on fire as though he were suffering from a fever. Anxious to charge the moment the artillery broke through the breastworks, Sam could barely keep his limbs still. To suffer the waiting, he let his mind jump to the future. Maybe he would be around the campfire tonight with his cousin Robert or Little Otter, sharing stories. He imagined returning to Baker Creek in triumph and seeing the look of pride on Ma's face. Or perhaps his body would lie waiting for a hero's burial, having died in a torrent of valor and glory.

Either way, Sam felt no fear. The fullness of his life as compared to his brothers made him feel ageless and wealthy beyond any measure of money. Then he thought of Paxton. Oh, if only his brother were here now. A pain, sudden and hard, gripped his heart, and he wanted to weep. He turned his eyes toward the sky. Then, without warning, a loud rattle of musketry mingled with the sharp crack of a hundred rifles. A heavy column of smoke rolled up from behind the barricade. Sam almost bolted forward, but Montgomery shouted, "Hold the position! We wait for orders."

Soon, word came that the Cherokee had swum the river and attacked the Red Sticks from the rear. Maybe Little Otter had been one of the warriors, or Crying Bear. The urge to join the fight made every inch of Sam's body twitch. If only he could have been with the Cherokee sneaking up on the Red Sticks.

To his amazement, orders came from Jackson to hold their position. Sam couldn't believe it until he saw a messenger with a white flag walking toward the barricade, sent to parley with the Red Sticks. Not much later, women and children began clambering over the barricade. With bundles on their backs, blankets over their heads, or babes in their arms, they straggled past the line of soldiers. A grim acceptance of their fate covered the women's faces. They were leaving their husbands, brothers, and sons for the last time. Goose bumps rose on Sam's arms as though the spirit of defeat was passing through him.

The sorrow for the women and children vanished the moment the drums announced the start of the assault.

Montgomery yelled, "Charge!"

Lightning struck Sam's body. With the flag in one hand and his musket in the other, he tore across the open expanse. His heart pumped in his chest while shot balls whistled by and arrows flew with a vengeance. A blinding, sulfurous haze floated over the barricade. Sam used his bayonet to block a porthole. On his right, Major Montgomery quickly took the rampart, and Sam grabbed for the topmost timber. In the next moment, Montgomery's body tumbled backward to the ground. Shot in the head, Sam's commanding officer was dead.

This was no time to stop. Sam waved the colors and quickly hurtled over to the other side. On the ground, he felt a slight sting to his groin and tried to spring forward, but something pulled between his legs. Glancing down, he saw an arrow sticking out of his thigh. He staked the flag in the ground and, with his fingers, probed for the barbed head and found it buried deep in his flesh. He tried to gently pull it out, but the angle was awkward, and the arrowhead refused to budge.

The Red Sticks retreated as more of the 39th poured over the ramparts. The fierce hand-to-hand fighting moved south to higher ground. Sam grabbed the next soldier over the breastworks.

"Get this out!" he shouted, pointing at his leg. The young private tugged at the shaft, but his hands slipped, causing blood to soak into Sam's white pantaloons. Then the man pulled harder. It stung like the devil, but the arrowhead stayed stuck. Sam raised his musket and shouted, "If you don't get it out this time, I'll smite you to the earth!"

The private shifted his position, and from a better angle, he gripped the shaft as close to Sam's groin as possible. This time, the young soldier braced his foot against Sam's torso, clenched his eyes shut, and with a quick, determined jerk, he yanked the arrowhead out. A horrendous pain radiated from the wound, but worse was the blood pouring out in waves of red. Sam pressed his hand over the wound, but it didn't stop the blood. If he didn't seek the surgeon's tent, he would bleed to death.

He handed the flag to the young soldier. "Don't lose this."

He hated to do it, but Sam crawled up and over the breastwork and walked stiff-legged to the surgeon's tent. His pantaloons were the color of a red-dyed blanket. They placed him on a table and slashed through the pants to reveal the wound. Sam raised up on one elbow. The gash was more than an inch long, and the edges of the tender white skin curled like ruffles where the barb had ripped through flesh. The surgeon's aide put a tourniquet above the wound and pulled tightly. It pinched and stung, and Sam gripped the aide's arm. Someone handed him a bottle. The whiskey brought momentary relief. The surgeon used a small hook to lift the bleeding artery. Sam took another greedy swig. The surgeon handed the hook to his aide and began to repair the tear with a curved needle and a thin waxy filament. By that time, either the whiskey or the loss of blood had worked its magic, and Sam could feel only a dull ache as the surgeon stitched the wound closed with black thread nearly the thickness of shoelaces. With a fresh dressing and another pair of pants, Sam limped from the tent.

Within a quarter hour, he felt refreshed and walked toward Colonel Williams, who was standing next to the general's horse. Sam addressed Colonel Williams. "I'm ready to rejoin the fight, sir."

Jackson looked down at Sam. Up close, the general's skin appeared sallow, and his left arm hung useless by his side. "Stay back," he told Sam.

"But, sir, I've hardly had my chance," Sam pleaded.

With a dismissive glance at Sam, Colonel Williams said, "Do not argue with your commander."

Jackson leaned down toward Sam with a slight grin on his lips and recognition in his eyes. "You carried the colors and were the first to breach the enemy line. Save your courage for the next battle."

The general sat up in the saddle again, wincing as he added, "It's a rout now. Let the Tennessee boys have their day."

Disappointed, all Sam could do was listen to the report of gunfire, the sporadic battle cries, and the terrible screams of the injured. As the afternoon wore on, the weary soldiers straggled back to the wagons, sometimes carrying in the wounded or dead. Sam couldn't stay away any longer. He moved closer to the barricade, now undefended. He walked through an opening where the ramparts had finally fallen and looked upon a row of bloodied and disfigured Red Stick corpses. A few held tomahawks in hand, and all had faces painted red or black. Some of the militia were going one by one to make sure each of the Red Sticks was dead. An older soldier thrust his bayonet into the soft hollow at the base of a throat. A groan escaped, followed by an awful gurgling noise.

"We shot them like the dogs they are," the soldier said.

A young smooth-faced boy bragged, "I gave one a mouth full of grapeshot."

Sam walked to the western banks. The river was running with blood and floating corpses. He had missed out on the real fighting. Having no stories to tell to prove his courage, he was shamed by the fact that others of lesser ability were now seasoned veterans while he remained chaste and inexperienced. And those militia men were likely ones who'd wanted to mutiny and return home, now bragging about their battlefield prowess. The disappointment hurt worse than the wound in his thigh.

A loud screech rang out, quickly followed by war whoops and a rifle shot that screamed like an angry hornet. The noise had come from the east, and Jackson galloped toward the commotion. Everyone who could, ran after the general.

A Cherokee spy had found the last of the Red Sticks hiding in a ravine leading down to the shore. Enough light was left to reveal branches and sticks creating a roof over a declivity in the ground, likely leaving enough room to shelter a good number of men. Some of the Cherokee stood around Jackson's horse. Sam went to be near the men in the 39th.

Jackson sent a soldier forward with a white flag. In a loud booming voice, the soldier called out to the Red Sticks, "Surrender, and your lives will be spared."

A murderous cascade of gunfire was the answer.

In the gloaming, Jackson sat tall and regal on his horse.

"The soft ground prevents the use of cannons, otherwise we'd blast them out. Under cover of night, how many of the Red Sticks will escape? The only way to defeat them is for brave men to fight for their country." The general lifted his sword. "Who will make this last charge?"

Sam looked at Colonel Williams, hoping the commander of the 39th would lead the assault, but the Colonel stayed quiet. Sam eyed the other senior officers, and to his dismay, none spoke. He couldn't stop from shaking and had to clench his jaw to keep his teeth from chattering. Major Montgomery would have answered without hesitation. He searched for anyone of rank to make a move, but none did.

To hell with them! Sam sprang forward with his gun, yelling, "Come on, men!"

He barreled down the embankment, his heart pounding against his ribs. The enemy's arrows and balls flew around him—this was his moment, his story to tell. A quick glance over his shoulder showed him at once that no one had followed. He called again for his men to join him. Almost upon the shelter, he slowed to level his musket. Before Sam could fire, he took a hit to his right forearm, rapidly followed by a jolt to his shoulder. The second ball had ripped through the sleeve of his jacket. Unable to fire or defend himself, Sam staggered back, out of range. His legs quivered then buckled under him. As he huddled on the ground, his shoulder and forearm burned with pain, and he felt the warmth of blood leaking from the wound in his groin.

Men from his platoon carried him to the surgeon's tent. Another mouthful of whiskey revived Sam while the ball in his forearm was easily extracted. He drank again before the surgeon turned to the shoulder wound, probing with his fingers for the shot ball. Sam groaned and twisted in agony. Worse than the stabbing pain were the awful noises. He tried not to look, but one glimpse confirmed his worst fears: his shoulder was now a sloppy mess of shattered bone and shredded muscle.

The surgeon turned away. "I can't get to it. No sense torturing him. Take him out with the others."

As he was lifted off the surgery table, a strange fear gripped Sam, and he strained to hear what was happening with the Red Stick holdouts. His heart lurched into his throat. If he had to die, he wanted it to be on the battlefield, but they took him to the area where the injured and dying soldiers had been placed. Sam attempted to sit up, but he fell back, exhausted and weak, on damp fallow ground. Under a moonless sky, he drifted in and out of a shadowy, pain-filled consciousness. Sometime later, a soldier appeared to take Sam's last will and testament.

"I leave all my worldly possessions to my mother."

The soldier placed a crude candlestick on the ground and scratched out the document in a hasty manner. He held Sam's hand to make a signature.

Sleep wouldn't return because his shoulder was on fire, and the wound in his groin throbbed mercilessly. His feet were stone cold, he couldn't feel his fingers, and flies crawled on his face where his skin was hot and sweaty. A sudden brisk wind brought on the shivers. Sam tried to lick his cracked lips, but his tongue wouldn't move. When he swallowed, it felt as though needles were lodged in his throat. He kept his breathing shallow, for the slightest movement brought on a misery worse than any he'd ever thought possible, as though at any moment, he would die from a wretchedness that had taken over every part of his body. With all measure of time lost, Sam drifted on the waves of a feverish nightmare that brought a heat that prickled his skin, followed by chills that shook his body in punishing jerks and spasms. Somehow, through that icy-hot torment, Sam heard a deep throaty clucking. When he opened his eyes, he saw the silhouette of a raven in a tree. The bird chortled again in a language Sam couldn't understand. A shadow crossed over the raven's silhouette. But shadows shouldn't appear on a moonless night. The raven's image returned and, with it, a soothing calmness. Sam's spirit rose, and his tortured body receded into the earth. Free now, he faced the raven up in the tree at eye level. After a moment, the raven grew larger, flapping its wings and bouncing on its legs before flying away, becoming the tiniest star in the sky.

A pleasant wind swept in with the promise of his destiny—a hero's death. With a lightness of heart, he ran toward it then glided above the sandy plains of Troy. Achilles, Hector, and Ajax were there. And Patroclus, he was nearest—warm and strong and brotherly. *No, not Patroclus.* It was Paxton by Sam's side now. They were standing in a river. A powerful, invigorating current pushed against his legs, and a whirlpool drew Sam toward deeper waters. Out of nowhere, a thunderclap boomed overhead. Then Paxton put his arm around Sam, holding him back from the whirlpool.

He whispered in Sam's ear, "No, brother, your time hasn't come. I will see you again when the grass is rising."

Another loud thunderclap was followed by someone with a voice clear and strong, calling like a bell in the distance.

"Houston."

General Jackson clapped his hands again. In his loudest voice, he yelled, "Houston!"

The young soldier's eyelids fluttered.

Jackson stared down at the surgeon. "Bring whiskey."

Clearly into his cups, the surgeon staggered back on his heels. "Sir, our supplies must be reserved for the ones who will live."

"That's an order!"

The surgeon stumbled off without a word.

The sharp pain in the general's bowels returned, and he bent down in the saddle, hugging his horse's neck. Andrew Jackson was suffering from the soldier's life—too little food, and what there was mostly unhealthy. But he'd learned to live with the debilitating diarrhea that often kept him from sitting a horse.

That soldier lying on the ground had been the one to answer the call for volunteers the night before. Seeing the young man's bloodied, mangled body lying unprotected from the bright morning sun made the general regret again that he'd called for a frontal assault on the hideout. Only while watching Houston be struck down did Jackson realize that fire would be the simplest way to drive out the Red Sticks. If he'd thought of it sooner, the young man would have been spared a painful injury.

Jackson had survived a similar wound, so maybe the young man would too.

The surgeon returned. A tin cup was brought to Houston's lips, and he revived a bit.

"Lieutenant Houston, your father was a revolutionary hero, as I recall." Jackson spoke with a loud but friendly tone.

The blue eyes brightened in a pale face.

"Your family shall hear of your courage, son."

Houston's eyes closed again, but his lips moved.

"What's he saying?"

The aide leaned in close to hear. "Something about grass rising."

Jackson straightened in his saddle. "I want this soldier attended to."

"But, General…" the surgeon started, but then he turned toward his aide with a nod.

A litter and two men came to carry Houston closer to the infirmary. Young Houston groaned when they lifted him.

Jackson glared down at the surgeon, commanding, "Do not take off his arm."

He knew all too well how quick the butchers were to amputate. Last September, after the duel with the Benton brothers, the doctors had wanted to take off his left arm. It might hang useless in his sleeve now, but the wound was mending, and he'd grown accustomed to the dull ache. It paled in comparison to the excruciating pain when his belly erupted in convulsions that forced him to double over in agony.

"Mark my words," Jackson said. "This young man has aspirations. He has the will to survive."

Colonel Coffey galloped toward them, yelling, "The Cherokee have found another hideout!"

And off the general went to deal with the last of the Red Sticks.

An excerpt from an article by Willoughby Williams on his recollections after the Battle of Horseshoe Bend:

"Disabled from further service, he (Sam) was sent back to Kingston with the sick and wounded. Robert H. McEwen and I met him some distance from Kingston, on a litter supported by horses. He was greatly emaciated, suffering at the same time from his wounds and the measles. We took him to the house of his relative, 'Squire John McEwen, brother of R. H. McEwen, where he remained for some time, and from thence he went to the house of his mother, in Blount County."

The shot ball stayed in Sam's shoulder for nearly a year. He traveled all the way to New Orleans, by way of Washington, DC, and through Virginia before he found a surgeon to remove it. The wounds in his groin and in his shoulder never fully healed and wept fluid for the rest of his life. In some of his letters, he would apologize for his handwriting when his arm bothered him.

His brother, Robert, returned to Virginia, where he committed suicide after a failed romance. This was sometime in 1814 or 1815. Martha McChesney is a fictional character.

Elizabeth Blair Paxton Houston died in 1831. At that point, she'd seen Sam go from being an up-and-comer in President Jackson's inner circle—serving two terms in Congress and winning the governorship in Tennessee—to a down-and-out political pariah. The fall from grace occurred after his young wife, Eliza Allen, abandoned him to return to her family in March 1829. The breakup wounded Sam to the core. He suffered a very public humiliation and resigned the governorship. He left Tennessee under a cloud of mystery, and neither Sam nor Eliza would ever disclose the reason their ninety-day marriage failed. It was a huge scandal, and the people who sided with her family burned Sam's image in effigy in Nashville.

James married and became a merchant in Nashville. Sam sued his oldest brother in 1832 for his share of their father's estate. James died in 1834.

John married and became a merchant in Memphis. The legend Marshall DeBruhl recounts is that John faked his own death to avoid some sort of scandal, swam across the Mississippi, and reemerged in Arkansas, later to hold an elected position in Izard County. John died in 1838.

William ended up in Arkansas. In 1854, he wrote to Sam, very timidly asking for a loan so that William could move his family to Texas. He died in Washington, DC, a few years after Sam.

Polly stayed in Tennessee. She married twice, and her son with the first husband died early. After her first husband passed, she married his nephew. She felt mistreated by her husbands' families and died in a mental institution in 1857.

Eliza married and inherited the farm at Baker Creek. Granny Peg lived with Eliza and died in Tennessee. Eliza and her husband eventually moved to Texas to be near Sam.

Oolooteka and the villagers of Hiwassee Island emigrated to Arkansas before the Removal of 1824. He would later become president of the Western Cherokee in Oklahoma after his brother Tahlunteeskee died.

The title comes from a letter Sam Houston wrote to Chief Bowles saying, "Brother… I will see you when the grass is rising." The letter resides at Rice University in the Fondren Library's collection entitled the "Franklin Weston Williams Collection of Sam Houston Material."

Chapter One - 1805

See *The Genuine Presbyterian Whine* article by William B. Bynum for background on the Presbyterian Worship in Eighteenth Century.

John Paxton, Sam's maternal grandfather, was granted a license to operate a tavern in 1761.

John Paxton's will was dated January 3, 1787, and specifically bequeathed "a wench named Peggy and three hundred pounds" to his son-in-law, Samuel Davidson Houston. It also bequeathed a half-acre lot in Lexington to each of his Houston grandsons alive at the time—James, John, and Robert. That is the first indication that Paxton was not the oldest son, as Rev. Samuel R. Houston stated in his article "The Biographical Accounts of the Houston Family.' Rev. Houston's account was the family tree used by the historians, but it is wrong. Since the maternal grandfather, John Paxton, died in 1789, and his will did not include Paxton, it's obvious that Paxton was not born before 1787. In addition, Rev. Houston stated that Paxton died around the age of maturity (21). If Paxton had been the oldest, he would have been dead before his father wrote his will in 1806. The wording of the Samuel Davidson Houston will reads, "… and my sons Paxton, Samuel, and William…" which is more evidence of the actual birth order of the three youngest sons.

On Nov. 25, 1799, Samuel and Elizabeth Houston sold land to Wm. Mackey north of Timber Ridge.

Robert Houston (Sam's paternal grandfather) sold the acre of land where the Old Stone Church was built to the Timber Ridge Presbyterian Congregation for five pounds. The church and cemetery were about one hundred yards from the Houston house.

On August 6, 1805, Samuel Davidson Houston appeared at the courthouse to defend himself against criminal charges brought by the Commonwealth of Virginia for the assault against Ann Henderson on the previous Sunday at the meetinghouse for the Timber Ridge Presbyterian congregation. The Major was acquitted, but four more lawsuits would drag on with his neighbors, Samuel and Daniel Lyle. Read more about the legal cases in *Jailing the Jerkers* by Doug Winiarski, University of Richmond.

Chapter Two - 1806

Sept. 1, 1806 Timber Ridge was sold to Mr. Kinneer for $1,000 by Samuel and Elizabeth Houston

Sept. 22, 1806 Samuel Houston signs his last will and testament.

On Nov. 5, 1806 a warrant was issued for Aaron Burr's arrest.

On Dec. 6, 1806 Burr was arrested in Kentucky, defended by Henry Clay, and acquitted.

Chapter Three - 1807

Land in Tennessee on Baker Creek surveyed on March 17, 1807.

On Nov. 6, 1807, the last will and testament of Samuel Houston was produced in court by Elizabeth Houston, James Houston, and John Houston.

Chapter Four - 1808

Elizabeth Houston had a copy of her father's will transcribed in January 1808 to prove ownership of Peggy before she left Virginia.

Land conveyance for four hundred nineteen acres in Blount County Tennessee from James Hogg to Elizabeth Houston (executor/administrator) was on Feb. 23, 1808.

Chapter Five - 1809

Robert F. Houston said that "Sam often visited my father's family. His mother had plenty, but was never wealthy. She had few slaves and did not want them." Taken from *The Biographical Accounts of the Houston Family* by Rev. Samuel R. Houston.

The Roane County Archives have the original Nicols & Shaifer documents with Sam Houston's signature from April 1809 to July 1809.

James Vann was killed in February 1809.

The John "Hell Jack Fire" Rogers family is documented in *Upon Our Ruins: A Study in Cherokee History and Genealogy* by Don L. Shadburn with John D. Strange, III, beginning on page 293.

James Marquis eloquently describes the scene when Sam rejected his brothers' demand to return to Baker Creek in *The Raven*, page 19.

Highwassee Garrison (21st May 1810) records include an entry saying "cash paid to John Jolly for pack horse hire, bringing money from Nashville - $7.00."

Chapter Six - 1810

The council of Oostinaleh (Ustinali) in April 18, 1810, abolished the custom of clan revenge. See *Myths of the Cherokee*, Mooney, page 86.

The prophet's reference to cats is in *Myths of the Cherokee*, Mooney, page 62.

Black Fox was chief of the Cherokee Nation at this time. See page 111, footnote 2, in the *Journal of John Norton*.

The Glass is described on page 47 in the *Journal of John Norton*.

The character Virginia Patsy has been reimagined from the young woman married to the son of John Boggs in the *Journal of John Norton* on page 148.

The character of Big Acorn has been reimagined from the man named Tasikayahi in the *Journal of John Norton* on page 152.

In a letter Sam Houston wrote to Joseph McMinn, dated June 19, 1823, he described his need for solitude.

The incident with Cusack (Cusick) is in *The Raven* by Marquis James on page 20, in Wisehart's biography on pages 11–12, and Haley's biography includes a brief description of the sheriff's fine on page 12.

Chapter Seven - 1811

The character of Tsali, the Prophet, is taken from the Cherokee prophet described in both appearance and influence in *Myths of the Cherokee*, Mooney, pp. 88–90.

The comet of 1811 was visible in the night sky from late August through the end of the year.

The New Madrid earthquakes occurred from Dec. 16, 1811, to February 1812.

Chapter Eight - 1812

The Sam Houston Schoolhouse Museum is located outside Maryville, TN.

Chapter Nine - 1813

Military Records titled *Prior to the Peace May 17, 1815*, Book 293, Remarks book 669, Mar. 2, Sam Houston enlisted; Book 537 (226) on Mar. 24, Sam Houston reported to Captain McClellan in Knoxville.

The story of the duel between Andrew Jackson and the Benton brothers is described by H. W. Brands in *Andrew Jackson: His Life and Times* on pages 188–192.

On his deathbed, Jackson sent for both Sam Houston and Thomas Hart Benton to come to him.

In 1956, when John F. Kennedy wrote *Profiles in Courage*, he included Senators Sam Houston and Thomas Hart Benton for voting against the Kansas-Nebraska Act in 1854.

Chapter Ten - 1814

The story of Private Wood's (spelled Woods in other records) court-martial and execution is detailed in *Andrew Jackson: His Life and Times* by H. W. Brands on pages 213–215, including excerpts from the letter Jackson wrote to Wood.

Marshall DeBruhl in *Sword of San Jacinto* recounts the legend about Sam threatening the young subaltern attempting to remove the barbed arrow in his groin, saying, "I will smite you to the earth."

Bibliography

ARTICLES & PAMPHLETS

A Review of the Battle of Horseshoe, and of the Facts relating to the Killing of Sixteen Indians, on the Morning after the Battle by the Orders of Gen. Andrew Jackson, political pamphlet compiled from Eaton's life on Jackson.
Cherokee Ball Play by James Mooney.
Coveted Lands: Agriculture, Timber, Mining, and Transportation in Cherokee Country before and after Removal by Vicki Bell Rozema.
Fort Hampton, the Riflemen, and the Mississippi Territory Frontier 1808–1817 by Mark Cole and Ben Hoksbergen.
"The Genuine Presbyterian Whine": Presbyterian Worship in the Eighteenth Century by William B. Bynum.
High Bridge Church and Cemetery, August 1928.
How Texas Won Her Freedom by Robert Penn Warren.
Jailing the Jerkers by Doug Winiarski.
Passports of the Southeastern Pioneers 1770–1823 by Dorothy Williams Potter.
Proceedings of the Rockbridge Historical Society, Volume XI.
Shakers and Jerkers, Two-Part Series, by Douglas L. Winiarski.

BOOKS

Sword of San Jacinto by Marshall DeBruhl.
The Raven by Marquis James (Pulitzer Prize).
Sam Houston: American Giant by M.K. Wisehart.
Sam Houston by James Haley.
Memoirs of Sam Houston by Charles Lester.
Life and Select Literary Remains of Sam Houston of Texas by Carey Crane.
My Master: The Inside Story of Sam Houston and His Times by His Former Slave Jeff Hamilton as told to Lenoir Hunt.

Sam Houston Boy Chieftain by Augusta Stevenson.

Sam Houston with the Cherokees, 1829-1833 by Jack Gregory and Rennard Strickland.

Brief Biographical Accounts of Many Members of the Houston Family compiled by Rev. Sam'l Rutherford Houston, D.D.

A History of Rockbridge County Virginia by Oren F. Morton.

Memory Days by Alexander Sterret Paxton.

Shenandoah Valley Pioneers and Their Descendants: A History of Frederick County, Virginia by T. K. Cartmell.

The Scots-Irish in the Shenandoah Valley by Billy Kennedy.

The Lexington Presbytery Heritage by Howard McKnight Wilson.

A Journey in Faith: The History of Timber Ridge Presbyterian Church by Taylor Sanders.

The Journal of Major John Norton, edited by Carl F. Klinck and James J. Talman, published by The Champlain Society.

Myths of the Cherokee by James Mooney.

Travels through North & South Carolina, Georgia, East & West Florida, the Cherokee Country, the Extensive Territories of the Muscogulges, or Creek Confederacy, and the County of the Chactaws; Containing an Account of the Soil and Natural Productions of Those Regions, Together with Observations on the Manners of the Indians by William Bartram.

Old Frontiers: The Story of the Cherokee Indians from Earliest Times to the Date of Their Removal to the West, 1838 by John P. Brown.

Cherokee Nation by Marion L. Starkey.

Cherokee Tragedy: The Ridge Family and the Decimation of a People by Thurman Wilkins.

Upon Our Ruins: A Study in Cherokee History and Genealogy by Don L. Shadburn with John D. Strange, III.

The War of 1812 by Francis F. Beirne, 1949

Journal of Travels into the Arkansa territory, 1819 by Thomas Nuttal, F.L.S.

Andrew Jackson: His Life and Times by H.W. Brands.

Andrew Jackson and Early Tennessee History by Samuel Gordon Heiskell.

The Falcon by John Tanner.

The Deerslayer by James Fenimore Cooper.

Things Fall Apart by China Achebe.

The One I Knew Best by Frances Hodgson Bennett.
The Agony and the Ecstasy by Irving Stone.

ARCHIVES/MUSEUM/HISTORIC SITES

Blount County Records, Blount County Courthouse, Maryville, Tennessee.

Briscoe Center at the University of Texas, Austin, Texas.

Chief Vann House State Historic Site, Georgia.

Forest Oaks, Natural Bridge, Virginia.

Franklin Weston Williams Collection of Sam Houston Material in Fondren Library at Rice University, Houston, Texas.

Funk Heritage Center, Reinhardt University, Georgia.

High Bridge Presbyterian Church and Cemetery, Natural Bridge, Virginia.

McClung Museum of Natural History & Culture, Knoxville, Tennessee.

National Archives, Washington, D.C.

Roane County Archives.

Rockbridge County Records, Rockbridge County Courthouse, Lexington, Virginia.

Sam Houston Memorial Museum, Huntsville, Texas.

Sam Houston Schoolhouse Museum, Maryville, Tennessee.

Sequoia Birthplace Museum, Vonore, Tennessee.

University of Tennessee Archives, Knoxville.

Washington & Lee University Library Special Collections & Archives, Lexington, Virginia.

Book Clubs

Discussion Questions

1. How did Major Houston's devotion to an unpaid commission in the Virginia militia affect the family's fortunes and Sam in particular?

2. What did Sam's relationship with Jerry say about the era (early 1800's) and Sam's character?

3. Many of his family and neighbors thought Sam was lazy, wild and disrespectful. Were their opinions justified?

4. How did Sam's time with the Cherokee influence his later life?

5. If Sam were alive today, what pop-psychology labels would we pin on him?

Acknowledgments

I couldn't have written this without the help of so many people. Jeff Bishop with the Funk Heritage Center pointed me to *The Journal of John Norton*. Doug Winiarski wrote the article "Jailing the Jerkers" that gave me the critical starting point. Mary Bell shared the stories about Sam's time as a schoolteacher. Robert Bailey, the Roane County archivist, provided records of the earliest known evidence of Sam's signature. The James Vann Plantation opened its reference library to me for research. The Rice University staff gave me access to the Williams collection of Sam's family correspondence. The Briscoe Center, the Sam Houston Memorial staff, and countless others provided material and direction. But it was my cousin's husband, Mickey Graham, who helped me see how Rev. Samuel Rutherford Houston had the birth order wrong in his biographical account of the extended Houston family.

For the editors, Sally J. Smith, Kelly Reed, and Bette James, thanks for helping me make this the best possible story. For my writing partners, Susan, Arwen, and Kathy, I appreciate all the times you read the early and often awkward drafts. For the beta readers, Carol and James, I am grateful for your encouragement.

A special thanks to my husband, family, and friends who endured years of my obsession with Sam Houston.

www.ingramcontent.com/pod-product-compliance
Lightning Source LLC
Chambersburg PA
CBHW021712190726

48289CB00008B/2489